THE GUNSMITH

452

Portrait of a Gunsmith

THE GUNSMITH

452

Portrait of a Gunsmith

J.R. Roberts

SPEAKING VOLUMES, LLC
NAPLES, FLORIDA
2019

Portrait of a Gunsmith

ISBN 978-1-64540-138-0

Chapter One

Santa Fe, New Mexico was peaceful and quiet. Having already seen to his horse, Eclipse's needs in a local livery, and got himself a hotel room, Clint Adams was walking around the town, enjoying the serenity. It was the first time in a long time he did not feel people were watching or plotting against him. There was the distinct possibility no one yet knew who he was, or that he was even in town.

He thought about registering under an assumed name but was not yet ready to start lying about who he was. So he would just enjoy these moments until somebody let the cat out of the bag. He got a room at a small place called The Cathedral Hotel, apparently because it used to be a cathedral.

He had been to Santa Fe before, but it felt different this time. Many of the storefronts had changed, and there now seemed to be many that were galleries, featuring some sort of artwork. He stopped in front of one window, which was filled with handmade pottery; another that was festooned with blankets of all sizes and colors; and still a third that had paintings on display, propped on easels. He had seen art galleries on his visits to New York City, but none in the West until now.

He passed several saloons, but didn't consider stopping anywhere until he reached a small café, and the savory aromas made their way to his nostrils. Immediately, he went inside, and found plenty of tables available, as it was between formal mealtimes.

"Señor," a pretty Mexican gal greeted him. Her peasant blouse was worn to show off her smooth, lovely shoulders. "A table?"

"Please," he said, "something away from the front."

"Of course, Señor," she said. "As you wish."

Since he was in New Mexico, not Old Mexico, he hadn't expected to stop and have Mexican food, but the heady aromas were irresistible.

"Would the Señor like to see a menu?" she asked. "We have many delicious Mexican dishes in our kitchen."

"And beer to wash it all down?" he asked.

"But of course."

"Good," he said. "I'll have a cold beer, and then bring me some of whatever it is I'm smelling."

"Oh si," she said, with a pretty smile, "the Señor will not be disappointed."

As he watched her prance away to the kitchen, he was thinking that he already was not disappointed.

***

She came back first with an ice-cold mug of beer, and then laden with plates up and down her arms. With obvious skill, she transferred dishes from her arms to the table without spilling a thing.

"Señor," she said, "red chili enchiladas, beef tacos, pork ribs in tomatillo sauce, some tortillas, and—"

"What's this?" Clint asked, pointing. "It looks amazing."

"That is *Pollo en Escabeche Oriental*."

"And that is?"

She laughed.

"It is Yucatan-style chicken and onion stew."

"And that's what I've been smelling, isn't it?" he asked.

"Oh, si," she said. "That is my papa's specialty."

"This is going to be good," Clint said. "I can tell."

"Enjoy, Señor," she said, "and let me know if you want anything else. My name is Norina."

"Thank you, Norina."

She walked away and left him to sample all of the delights on the table.

While he ate, he was surprised that no one else entered the small café. But he didn't mind eating alone, with no one staring at him.

He started with the chicken and onion stew, found it delicious, and moved on to the other dishes. They were all

3

exploding with flavors he had sampled only a few times before, in Mexico.

There were different kinds of artwork on display around the room. Homemade pots on shelves, blankets nailed to the walls, but the items that really attracted his attention were the paintings.

They covered one wall, canvasses of all sizes and shapes, featuring many colors. They were all depictions of houses, mountains, flatlands, desert plants, and to his untrained eye it seemed to him that the artist was the same one in each.

He was halfway through his meal when Norina returned, carrying another mug of beer.

"Thank you," he said. "Can you stay a moment?"

"Of course, Señor," she said. "As you wish."

"Tell me about that wall," he said, pointing to the display of paintings.

"Ah Señor," she said, "you have an eye for art!"

Chapter Two

"All those paintings are by the same artist," Norina told him. "She lives here in Santa Fe, and is a wonderful, talented lady."

"What's her name?"

"She is called *La Dama Artistica.*"

"And that is?"

"The Artistic Lady."

"Are these paintings for sale?" he asked.

"She has a gallery in town," Norina said. "Papa displays her paintings here, but you must go to her gallery if you wish to purchase them."

He continued to eat as they talked. She warmed to her subject and actually sat down with him.

"Have some of this," he said.

She looked behind her at the kitchen door and said, "I really shouldn't, but . . ." She reached out and snagged a taco, began to eat it.

"How well do you know this lady?" he asked.

"I know her very well," she said. "I met her when I was a little girl."

"And other than La Dama Art—art—"

"*Artistica*," she said.

"Yes, other than that, does she have a name?"

"Lucinda."

"Ah," he said, "A pretty name."

"Si."

"And Norina is a pretty name," he added.

"Gracias."

"What does it mean?"

"It means 'bright,'" she said.

"Well, that seems accurate," he said. "You have a bright smile, and you seem like a bright girl."

She stood up and said to him, "I am not a girl, I am a woman."

He realized that he had somehow insulted her.

"Yes, you are," he said. "You are a lovely woman. I'm sorry if I insulted you."

"I—I must go back to the kitchen."

He thought he saw tears in her eyes as she turned and walked away. He wondered if there was something else going on with her.

As he was approaching the end of the sumptuous meal, a family walked in the door and was shown to a table by Norina. There was a father and mother with two small children, a boy who looked about five, and a three-year-old girl. They conversed with Norina in Spanish, and during that she seemed to have recovered from her previous mood. He almost thought of her reaction as a snit, but felt that would also be insulting.

She apparently took their order, also in Spanish, and went to the kitchen to tell her father what to cook. Then she came back over to Clint's table.

"Can I do something else for you?" she asked.

"Yes," he said, "you can forgive me for insulting you. I didn't mean to do that."

She waved a hand and said, "Do not worry. It was not just what you said. Please, do not worry."

"All right," he said. "Thank you."

"We have some flan for dessert."

"I'll take it," he said, "with some coffee."

"Mexican coffee?"

"What's the difference?"

"Three ounces of coffee liqueur, three ounces of tequila, cinnamon dust and two cups of coffee."

"Bring it," he said.

She cleared the table of the plates, then brought him a small bowl of flan, and a mug of Mexican coffee.

While he ate his dessert, he continued to examine the paintings on the wall. There was something . . . arresting about the images. No, maybe not the images, but the way they were presented.

Norina brought out the plates of food for the family, who all dug in enthusiastically.

"How was the coffee?" she asked.

"Wonderful," Clint said. "You tell your father that everything was great."

He settled the bill with her, and added something extra for the service, and because he had insulted her, somehow.

"Are you going to go to Lucinda's gallery?" she asked, as he stood up.

"I think I am," he said. "What's it called?"

"The same thing she is called," Norina said. "'La Dama Artistica.'"

"Where is it?"

"Just go out our door, turn left and walk five blocks. It's at the beginning of the plaza."

"Thank you, Norina," he said.

She walked to the door with him, put her hand on his arm. He studied her face. She was, indeed, a woman and a beautiful one at that, probably around twenty-two.

"Let me know what you think of it," she said. "I am always here."

"I will," he said. "I'll see you soon."

He turned left and started walking.

Chapter Three

He strolled rather than walk the five blocks toward the central plaza of Santa Fe, where not only artists but Indians displayed their wares on the street. This was something that had blossomed there since his last visit.

He could see the plaza was crowded with people who worked there, and with people who were simply shopping when he reached the gallery. Over the door, on a piece of wood, was written LA DAMA ARTISTICA. In the window were paintings that looked like the ones he saw in the café, but there were also portraits, of both white men and women, and Indians.

He went inside.

There were several customers there, looking at the paintings that were displayed on easels and on the wall. He walked around the room slowly, examining the works. Lucinda's talent seemed to increase the more he studied them. Perhaps he was seeing them in some sort of order, from early in her career until now. That would explain why the paintings seemed to be getting better and better.

He looked around, but didn't see anyone who looked like an artist. Then a woman came through a doorway, appearing every inch like an artist. Her clothing was colorful, voluminous, with no hint of what the body beneath was like. But from the neck up she was beautiful, with smooth, dark skin, red lips, dark eyes and shiny, midnight black hair, parted in the center.

She approached a customer and handed her a small square package wrapped in brown paper. It looked like one of the smaller paintings.

After that she spoke to a couple more customers, one conversation in English, another in Spanish. Then she walked around behind her counter and began to go through some papers.

Clint walked around until the last customer left, and it was only he and the woman he assumed was Lucinda.

He walked over to the counter and she looked up at him with those haunting, dark eyes.

"Can I help you?"

"Norina sent me here," he said.

She smiled, and her beauty increased.

"That sweet girl."

"I was eating there and looking at your paintings on the wall," he said. "They're . . . breathtaking."

"Well, thank you."

"I assume you're Lucinda," he said, "'La Dama Artistica?'"

"That is me," she said. "And you are . . .?"

"My name's Clint Adams."

She stared at him for a few moments, expressionless, and then asked, "The Gunsmith?"

"That's right."

"I hadn't heard you were in town."

"I only arrived this afternoon," he said. "Checked into a hotel, got something to eat."

"And came here?"

"Yes."

"Why?"

"I told you," he said. "I find your work impressive. I wanted to meet you."

She studied his face, which gave him time to study her more closely. Norina said she met Lucinda when she was a young child. The lines at the corners of her eyes and mouth gave Lucinda's age away as late forties, possibly early fifties. But still a beautiful woman.

"Do you want to buy a painting?" she asked.

"I'm afraid not," he said. "I spend most of my time on horseback. I really have no place to put a painting."

"Do you know art?"

"No," he said, "although I've been to some galleries in New York."

Now her eyebrows went up.

"New York City?" she asked. "You mean . . . Manhattan?"

"That's right," he said. "I think your paintings are every bit as good as anything I've seen there."

"Well . . ." She seemed to become breathless. "I don't know what to say—"

She was interrupted when a man came through the same door she had. He was tall, dark-haired, with grey at the temples, and looked decidedly Mexican.

"Who is this?" he asked, immediately.

"Carlos, this is Clint Adams," she said. "Mr. Adams, my husband, Carlos."

"Nice to meet you," Clint said.

"What do you want?" The man glared at him. "What are you doing here with my wife?"

"Just talking to her about her work," Clint said. "I saw some paintings in a café where I ate—"

Now the man glared at his wife.

"They still have your work on the walls of that cheap restaurant?" he demanded.

"Now wait a minute—" Clint said, but the man cut him off.

"No, you wait a minute!" he snapped. "You must leave, we are closing."

Clint looked at the woman.

"I am sorry," she said. "You should go."

"You do not need to apologize for me!" the man snapped at her.

As Clint left, he thought he heard the sound of a slap.

Chapter Four

Clint didn't like the idea of leaving the art gallery and the artist with a man who might have been slapping her. His first thought was to turn around and go back in, but at that moment he heard the door lock from the inside. He tried to look in the window on the door, but the curtain had been pulled.

When he walked around to look in the display window, he could see the interior of the gallery, but there was nobody there. He figured he was just going to have to keep his nose out of the business of a married couple.

He turned and walked away.

***

Sometime later, after strolling around the plaza a bit, he stopped in a little saloon on the other side of the square. It was doing a fairly brisk business, but he found a spot at the bar easily and ordered a beer from the tall, thin, pasty white bartender. The man looked as if he had never been in the sun in his life.

"Thanks," he said, accepting the mug and paying for it.

"Stranger, huh?" the man said.

"How can you tell?"

"Well, you don't know anybody here," the bartender said. "This is pretty much a saloon that's frequented by the same people. You just come out of the plaza?"

"That's right."

The bartender nodded.

"That's the only time strangers in town find us," he said.

"So you know everybody in Santa Fe?"

"I know a lot of people," the man said. "That's what happens when you tend bar."

"What can you tell me about an artist named Lucinda?"

"Ah," he said, "you mean 'La Dama Artistica,' on the other side of the plaza."

"That's right."

"Whataya wanna know about her?" he asked. "She's a talented lady."

"Her husband," Clint said. "What's he like?"

"Ah, Carlos Montalban," the bartender said. "He's a mean man—meaner still when he gets drunk."

"Does he beat her?"

"Probably."

"Does he drink in here?"

"Never," the man said. "We're too low class for him. He thinks he's a—whataya call it—ari—astra—"

15

"Aristocrat?" Clint helped.

"That's it!"

"You talkin' about Carlos?" another man at the bar said.

"Yeah, Dick, this feller was askin' about him."

"You don't wanna mess with him, Mister," Dick said. "He's just bloody mean."

"But does he beat his wife?" Clint asked.

"I've seen her with a bruise or two, yeah," Dick said.

"Men who do that are usually cowards," Clint said. "Beat women because they can't beat men."

"Oh, he's beat plenty of men," Dick said, "'specially men he thinks are talkin' to his wife when they shouldn't be."

"So he's the jealous type, huh?"

"Oh yeah," Dick said. "He's killed one man I know of out of jealousy, and got away with it."

"How?"

"He's got a lot of friends in town," Dick said.

"But not in here?"

Dick and the bartender laughed.

"Jesus, he wouldn't be caught dead in here," Dick said. "That right, Nate?"

"You said it," Nate, the bartender, agreed.

"Take my advice, Mister," Dick said. "If you're interested in his wife, find somebody else. In fact, there's a whorehouse on the end of town. Nice girls."

"No," Clint said, "I'm not interested in any whores, and not in anybody's wife, either. I was just interested in her paintings."

"Ah," Nate said, "you had a run in with Carlos, already, didja?"

"Sort of," Clint said. "Kicked me out of the gallery. As I left, I thought I heard him slap her."

"Yeah, that'd be Carlos," Dick said. "I guess maybe you better find yourself another artist."

"But I like her paintings," Clint said. "I wasn't finished looking at them or talking to her about them."

"Well, that's up to you, Mister," Dick said. "Can't say I didn't warn you."

"Much obliged for the warning, friend."

"You want another beer?" Nate asked.

"No," Clint said, "I'll just finish this one."

The bartender nodded and moved on down the bar to serve somebody else.

It seemed like Santa Fe might not be the nice, quiet, peaceful town he was thinking it was. Of course, he could mount up and ride out, forget all about La Dama Artistica. But he couldn't do that until morning. He needed a good night's sleep in a hotel bed first.

Chapter Five

It was too early to go to his hotel and turn in, so he walked back to the café he'd eaten in earlier, to see if it was still open and if Norina was there. He had met Lucinda for a moment, and yet he found himself worrying about her.

The front door of the café was open, but when he looked inside, nobody was sitting there. He entered and was about to walk to the kitchen door when Norina came out.

"Oh," she said, "I thought you were a customer. You are not back here to eat again, are you? So soon?"

"No, that's not it," he said. "Do you have time to talk?"

She waved her arms and said, "All I have is time."

He walked to a table and said, "Please, sit with me a few minutes."

She came over and sat.

"I went to that gallery you told me about." He pointed to the paintings. "Lucinda's."

"You met her?"

"Yes."

"Are you in love with her, already?"

"Not after only a few minutes," he said. "We got to talking and then her husband came in and kicked me out."

"Carlos." She spat the name out like it was a bad word.

"You don't like him?"

"There is not a woman in town who likes Carlos."

"And what about the men?"

"The men all think he is wonderful."

"A man who beats his wife?"

"She is his wife, is she not?" Norina asked. "Does that not give him the right to beat her?"

"I don't think so."

"Then you are different from other men."

"I like to think so."

"Señor," she said, "why did you want to talk to me?"

"I'm worried," he said. "When I left the gallery, it sounded like he was already slapping her for talking to me."

"That is because you are *muy guapo*," she said.

"What does that mean?"

She looked away and said, "Very handsome." Then she turned back. "And he is *muy celosa*—very jealous. He has killed men for looking at her."

"And gotten away with it?"

"Si. He is a big man in Santa Fe."

"That's too bad," he said, standing up.

"What are you going to do?" she asked.

"I'm going to talk to her again."

"Tonight?"

"No," he said, "probably not until tomorrow."

"What will you do tonight?"

"I don't know," he said. "Go back to my hotel, I guess."

"Not get drunk in a saloon?"

"No."

"Then you are very different from other men," she pointed out.

"Maybe."

He started for the door, and she stood up quickly.

"I will be closing in one hour," she said. "Would you come back and walk me home, *por favor*?"

"Sure," he said. "Why not? One hour."

He left, headed for his hotel.

***

When he returned an hour later Norina smiled at him as he entered. She was sweeping the floor.

"I am finished," she said. "We can go."

"What about your father, the cook?"

"He left already, went to the saloon where he will drink until he is drunk. Then he will come home and sleep. In the morning I will have to force him to wake up."

"That's too bad."

"It is because he is a man," she said. "Wait. I will get the key."

He waited out front for her, and when she reappeared, she was wearing a shawl over her shoulders. She closed the door and locked it.

"I live this way."

They started to walk together as dusk was falling.

"Do you have trouble walking home?"

"Sometimes," she said, "there are men who . . . who think because I served them food and talked to them, they can . . . well, you know."

"I think so."

"Before my Mama died three years ago, she told me that men are like that because it is . . . *como se dice* . . . their natural?"

"Their nature," he corrected.

"Si, that was it," Norina said. "It is their nature."

"I'm afraid your mother was right," Clint said, "at least, when it comes to a pretty girl."

"I am not so pretty," she said. "You saw Lucinda. She is *muy Boninta*."

"Well, I think you're muy bonita too, Norina."

"Gracias . . . I do not know your name."

"Clint."

"Gracias, Clint. My house, it is not far now."

Chapter Six

Norina's home was in a part of town where there were many small, adobe houses. She led Clint up to the front door of one of them and put the key in the lock.

"It's very dark inside," she said. "Would you come in with me?"

"Sure."

He followed her in, waited while she groped around in the dark, presumably for a lamp.

There was a rustle of some sort, then her voice came out of the darkness.

"There's an oil lamp just to your left," she said. "Would you light it for me?"

He reached out cautiously, touched the lamp, then turned and lit a match, touched it to the wick. The room was bathed in a warm, gentle light. When he turned back, he saw her standing naked, shadows flickering on her skin. Now he knew the rustle he had heard was her dress coming off.

He caught his breath. She was young and beautiful, her body smooth and curvy. In the yellow light of the lamp her large nipples looked very brown.

"Norina," he said, "your father—"

"I told you," she said. "He's in a saloon, getting drunk. He will not come home for hours. Please . . . I want you."

"I'm very flattered," he said, "but you're so young—"

"I am twenty."

"Even younger than I thought," he groaned. "And so beautiful . . ."

"Then come to me," she said, extending her arms.

"I can't," he said, his mouth dry and his body betraying him. "I can't do it . . . not here, not now . . . I'm sorry . . . you don't know how sorry . . ."

He backed up to the door and left the naked girl still reaching for him . . .

***

Clint walked back to his hotel, feeling like a fool and a lecher. The girl was so willing, but she was so damn young. Of late he'd found himself having a problem being with young women. Not a physical problem, but a mental one. It just didn't seem right.

During the walk to the hotel his erection softened, thankfully. He had almost been unable to leave that house, his body wanted so much to reach out and grab her.

Before going to the hotel, he stopped in a saloon for a drink . . .

***

When he finally got to his hotel, he was feeling better. A shot of whiskey and a beer had done the trick. But the look the desk clerk gave him as he went up the stairs alerted him. Something was brewing . . .

He walked down the hall and approached his door, stopped just outside and put his hand on it. Someone was inside. He hoped it wasn't Norina. On the other hand, he hoped it wasn't somebody with a gun.

Slowly, carefully, he turned the doorknob, and then slammed the door open.

The woman inside turned and looked over her shoulder, startled, her beautiful eyes very wide.

"Oh!" she said.

"I'm sorry I scared you," he said, "but . . . what are you doing here?"

Lucinda, La Dama Artistica, turned to face him. She was still wearing the same dress as in her gallery, with a shawl over it. There was still no hint as what her body was like beneath it.

"I—I came here to apologize."

"Apologize . . . for what?" he asked.

"Can we . . . close the door?" she asked. "I do not want to be seen . . ."

He closed the door and turned to face her again.

"I am sorry for the way my husband spoke to you," she said. "Carlos is a jealous man."

"We weren't doing anything but talking," he said.

"I know," she said, "I told him that. I finally calmed him down after you left."

"After he slapped you?"

She touched her cheek quickly, then dropped her hand just as quickly.

"It was nothing."

"And what if he finds out you were here?"

"He will not."

"The desk clerk—"

"He is my cousin," she said. "He will not tell."

"Well . . . you better leave, anyway," Clint said. "I accept your apology."

"I—before I leave." She abruptly sat on the bed. "I wanted to ask you something."

He hoped it wasn't going to be the same thing Norina had asked him.

Chapter Seven

"I would like to paint you."

That surprised him.

"Why?"

"I know who you are," she said. "It would be an honor to paint the portrait of the Gunsmith."

"I don't know . . ." he said. "What would your husband think of that?"

"I would explain it to him," she said. "He will understand. Carlos is a jealous man, but he is not stupid. This would be my masterpiece."

He'd been called a lot of things in his time, but that was a first.

"I'm very flattered, Lucinda, but sitting for a portrait, that would take time—"

"Not so very much," she assured him. "Is there another reason?"

"Well . . . that name," he said, "I'm not . . . I don't go around calling myself that."

"Are you ashamed of it?"

"Not ashamed," he said. "It's hard to explain."

She stood up and walked to the table next to the bed, picked up the slender book that was there. She held it up so he could see the title. It was a dime novel, with a drawing of what was supposed to be him on the front. On the top it said THE GUNSMITH, A LEGEND OF THE WEST. Underneath was the author's name. It wasn't one he recognized: Edward Minturn. (He later discovered this was a pseudonym of Ned Buntline).

In the past he had avoided such books, but lately he'd grown curious about what people were writing, so he had decided to read this one.

"This does not look like you are ashamed," she said. "But this . . . this cover . . . She turned it around and looked at it. "That is not you."

"I don't usually pay attention to those," he told her. "I was just curious . . ."

She dropped the book onto the table, like it was a dead fish.

"I would do you justice," she promised.

"Lucinda—"

"Please," she said, "just think about what I have said, and do not leave town until we talk again?"

He took a deep breath, let it out in a sigh.

"Yes, all right," he said. "We'll talk about it again—as long as your husband doesn't mind."

"He will not," she said. "I assure you. I will say good-night, now."

She started for the door, but he stopped her.

"Let me check the hall for you, make sure it's empty."

"Gracias," she said.

He opened the door, peered out, looked both ways, and then stepped aside.

"Okay," he said.

She stepped out, then turned to face him again.

"Please," she said, "give it serious thought."

"I will," he said. "I promise."

With that she walked down the hall and disappeared down the stairs. He closed the door and locked it, then walked to the bedside table and looked at the dime novel cover, shaking his head.

***

He slept well and woke rested. He thought again of the two women he had been alone with last night. He thought either one would have given him a most pleasant night. Norina was beautiful, but too young. Lucinda was certainly old enough, but she was married. He had always promised himself he would avoid sleeping with married women, but of late seemed to be having difficulty keeping that promise. He was kind of proud of himself for having walked away from the naked Norina.

On the other hand, would he have walked away from Lucinda if she had made the same offer to him that the younger girl had? He hoped so . . .

29

He left the hotel that morning and went in search of someplace else to have breakfast other then Norina's café. He really wasn't prepared to face her again.

He found a place a few streets in the opposite direction, so that he was nowhere near her café. Over a very American breakfast of steak-and-eggs he thought again about Lucinda's offer to paint him. He had to admit, having seen her work, he was curious about how such a portrait would look. If her husband wasn't dead set against it, where was the harm?

Well, he *had* promised her they would talk again about it. So, after breakfast he walked to her gallery.

***

He stopped just outside and peered in the window. She was alone, standing behind her counter, examining something intently. He looked both ways on the street for her husband, then inside again. Finally, he took a deep breath and entered.

Chapter Eight

When she looked up and saw him, it was evident how pleased she was.

"Mr. Adams!"

"Just call me Clint," he said, looking around. "Is your husband here?"

"Carlos is out," she said. "I was just doing some paperwork until customers came in. But if you want to talk, I can lock the door and close for a short time."

"I don't want to cost you business."

"Oh, don't worry about that," she said. "My business is very . . . fluid. At the moment, I have time on my hands. Here, let me lock the door."

She came out from behind the counter and moved in a flurry of billowing skirts. She locked the door, and turned the OPEN sign to CLOSED.

"There, now we can talk," she said. "Come in the back to my studio."

"Lucinda—" he started, but she was gone and he had no choice but to follow her through the doorway.

He was surprised to find himself not in a studio, but a storeroom. There were barrels on the floor, items on shelves lining the walls, and some canvasses on the floor and on easels.

"In here!" she called.

He saw another doorway in a side wall and walked to it. When he peered in, he saw a very different room, a bright room with sunlight coming in through a back window, and a window in the roof. There were several easels set up and the walls were white.

"I'm impressed," he said, stepping inside.

"When we bought this building, one of the first things we did was add this room into the back."

Clint walked to the window and looked out at the horizon. There was a lot of flat ground, and mountains in the distance.

"If you agree to sit for me, I would paint you in here," she said.

He turned, saw her standing in front of a white wall, her hands clasped in front of her, watching him.

"Have you decided?"

"I've almost made up my mind."

"If you like," she said, "I can show you some other portraits I have painted?"

"That would be helpful."

"A moment."

She walked to the doorway, went into the storage area, then came back carrying several canvases. He hurried to help her, taking several from her.

"Thank you," she said. "Just set them against the wall."

He did, putting some facing out, some facing the wall. She set down the ones she was holding then, one by one, turned them all around.

"There."

There were six of them, the canvases of differing sizes and shapes. But what they all had in common was that they were portraits. Six people were looking out at him.

"These are very good," he said. "Who are they?"

She pointed to an older man's face and said, "That is the mayor. Or, he was the mayor when I painted it. He has since been replaced, and retired."

Clint walked from canvas to canvas, finally stopping in front of the fifth one. It was a young girl with dark skin and very black hair.

"Is that . . ." he started.

"Yes," she said, "that is Norina. She was sixteen when I painted that."

The other portraits were men and women of different ages. Lucinda said they were all citizens of Santa Fe who had agreed to sit for her.

"Why them?" he asked. "Why did you choose to paint them?"

"Because the lines and planes of their faces were extraordinary," she said, "different from everyone else." She looked at him. "Like yours."

"Mine? What's different about mine?"

"You have a strong jaw, good cheekbones, intense eyes . . . you will make my most compelling subject, yet."

"How would you do it?" he asked. "Sitting?"

"No," she said, "standing, I think."

"These people are just faces."

"I want to do all of you," she said, "including your gun. This would not be a portrait of Clint Adams, but a portrait of the Gunsmith."

"And what would you do with it when it's finished?"

"I could give it to you," she said, "but you have already said you have nowhere to put it."

Suddenly, he thought about his friend Rick Hartman's saloon and gambling hall in Labyrinth, Texas. It grew as the town grew. He wondered if Rick would want it?

"All right," he said.

"All right? You mean—"

"Yes," he said, "I mean, let's do it."

She clapped her hands and said, "*Excelenete*!"

Chapter Nine

"I'll just need one thing before we start," he went on.

"I will need many more than that," she said, "but what is it you need?"

"I need to talk to your husband."

"Carlos? Why?"

"I want his okay on this."

"He does not tell me who to paint," she said, tightly.

"He's a jealous man," Clint said. "I want to assure him that I'm only interested in his wife as an artist, not as a woman."

She stared at him.

"Did I just insult you?" he asked. "You're a beautiful woman, Lucinda—"

"You did not insult me," she said. "My husband has an office several streets from here, before you get to the plaza. He should be there now."

"What kind of an office?" Clint asked. "What does your husband do?"

"He is a lawyer."

***

They agreed that Clint would go and talk to Carlos while she got herself ready to work.

Clint left the La Dama Artistica gallery and walked along the street until he found what he was looking for. A shingle hanging above a door read: CARLOS MONTALBAN, ATTORNEY.

He opened the door and stepped inside.

Lucinda had told him that her husband had a secretary. "Her name is Ayesha." She pointed to one of the canvases against the wall. "That is her."

It was another portrait of a dark-skinned, dark-haired Mexican beauty who appeared, age-wise, to be somewhere between Lucinda and Norina.

Now, as he entered and a woman looked up from her desk, he saw that Lucinda's painting did not do the woman justice. She was so beautiful she left him breathless for a full minute.

"Yes?" she asked in a husky voice. "Can I help you?"

He licked his lips, tried to speak, then repeated the process. Finally, he said, "I'm here to see Mr. Montalban."

"I am afraid he is very busy," she said. "May I tell him who you are?"

"Yes," he said, "my name is Clint Adams."

"And what does this concern?" she asked. "Do you need a lawyer?"

"I want to talk to him about La Dama Artistica."

"His wife?"

"Yes."

"Señor," she said, "Carlos does not like to talk about this wife . . . with other men."

"Please," he said, "just tell him I'm here and let's see what happens."

"Very well," she said. "Please wait."

When she stood, he could see she was very tall, and wearing a multi-colored dress that hung down to her ankles. It reminded him of the ones he had seen Lucinda wear, only not as loose."

When she came back several minutes later, she had a stunned look on her face.

"He says he will see you," she said, seating herself. "Please, go in."

She studied her desktop, as if trying to see if something was out of place.

Clint went through the door and into the office. Carlos Montalban was sitting behind a very large desk. The last time he had seen a desk that large was in Fort Smith, Arkansas. Judge Isaac Parker had been seated behind that one.

He wondered if Carlos Montalban knew that?

"Mr. Adams." Montalban got up from behind the desk, came around and approached Clint. He was wearing

37

a black suit and a boiled white shirt. He extended his hand, Clint shook it.

"Mr. Montalban—"

"Before you start," Montalban said, "please allow me to apologize for my behavior yesterday. It was inexcusable."

"That's all right," Clint said, as the lawyer returned to his desk. "We all have bad days."

"Indeed," Montalban said, "and yesterday was quite bad. Now, what can I do for you?"

Clint decided not to sit down. Hopefully, this conversation would not take very long.

"I would like your permission to pay your wife to paint my portrait."

The man studied him for a few seconds, expressionless, and Clint thought he could see something lurking beneath the surface. But then it passed, and the man smiled.

"I do not tell my wife what subjects she may or may not paint, Señor," Montalban said. "Have you spoken to her?"

"This morning."

"And it was her idea to paint you, no?"

"I'd pay her."

Montalban waved his hand.

"That does not matter," he said. "She must be already preparing her studio, no?"

"I suppose—"

"Mr. Adams," Montalban said, "I am sure you will approve of the portrait my wife will paint of you."

"Then we have your permission?"

"It is not necessary," Montalban said, "but you have my blessing."

Chapter Ten

Clint left Montalban's office and headed back to the La Dama Artistica gallery. He wondered which Carlos Montalban was the real one, the jealous, raging man from yesterday, or the calm, logical man he met today. Maybe Lucinda would know.

When he got back to the gallery, the front door was unlocked, and Lucinda was back behind the counter. She was in the act of wrapping a canvas for a middle-aged female customer, who thanked her and left with it.

"Good sale?" he asked.

"A small one," she said. "Did you see Carlos?"

"I did," Clint said. "He says we have his blessing."

"He actually said that? Blessing?"

"Yes."

"That's not like him."

"I was wondering about that," Clint said. "Did I meet the real Carlos yesterday, or today?"

"The real one is probably somewhere between the two," Lucinda said. "But that doesn't matter. Can we start the portrait tomorrow?"

"Whatever you say," Clint told her. "I'm at your disposal."

"I'll need you for a few hours," she said, "so make sure you eat a hearty breakfast."

"And what do you want me to wear?"

"Your gun," she said. "After that you can wear whatever you like. Just be here early."

"And what about your business while you're painting me?" he asked.

"Do not worry," she said. "I will have someone here to handle sales."

"Okay, then," he said. "See you in the morning."

He left her gallery and went to buy a new shirt.

***

After Clint left Carlos Montalban's office, Ayesha stood, locked the door, and went into Montalban's office, closing that door, as well.

As she came around his desk, he turned sideways so his legs were not beneath the desk. She got on her knees in front of him and started to undo his trousers.

"Who was he?" she asked, sliding his pants off.

"His name is Clint Adams," he said.

"I know. He told me that." She took his underwear off next. His big penis was just sort of lying along his thigh.

"Come on, Ayesha, you know the name," he said, as she took his cock in her hand and started to stroke it.

41

"He's a Gunsmith."

"Ah," she said, as his penis began to stiffen, "that is why the name was familiar. What did he have to say about your wife?"

Montalban groaned as his cock hardened and she expertly manipulated it in her hand.

"She is painting his portrait."

"Really?" she asked. "And you don't mind?"

"As long as you are doing that," he said, "I don't mind."

His cock was now jutting up from his crotch, red and demanding.

"And what if I do this?" She leaned forward, licked the head, took it into her mouth, wet it, and then swooped down to engulf his cock in her hot mouth.

"Ah, yesssss . . ." he said. "Do that!"

***

Clint bought a blue shirt.

He didn't bother replacing his hat or buying new Levis.

He left the store with his shirt wrapped in brown paper and decided it might be time to stop for lunch and see Norina again.

***

The café was doing a scant business, with only two tables occupied. Norina was bringing plates to one table. After she set them down, she turned and saw Clint in the doorway.

"Why are you here?" she asked.

"Somebody told me you've got the best food in town," he said.

"You wish a table?"

"Yes."

"Take any one you like."

She turned and went back to the kitchen. He saw that he had some fences to mend.

He walked to the back and sat at a table. The other diners looked at him, then turned their attention to their meals, again. There were two men sitting together, and one alone. All three looked like town merchants.

When Norina came back out from the kitchen, she put a beer on one of the tables, then walked over to Clint.

"What may I get you?" she asked, stiffly.

"How about a smile?" he asked.

"I am here to take your order," she said, "not to smile."

"Come on, are you mad at me about last night?"

"You . . . left me standing there . . . feeling foolish," she told him.

"I'm really sorry, Norina," he said, "but I just . . . couldn't take advantage of you at that moment."

"You weren't," she said. Then she suddenly sat down. "I suppose I should apologize to you for putting you in that position. If you do not find me desirable—"

"That's not it, at all," he said. "You're a lovely, girl, and very desirable. You're just . . . young."

"Well . . . I can't help that."

"Aren't there any boys here, young men, who you . . . like?"

"No," she said, "I do not have time for that. And my father . . . he is very strict. I suppose that was why I thought perhaps you, a stranger . . . and my father was in the saloon . . . I just thought I would . . . how did you put it . . . take advantage?"

"How about we agree that neither of us has anything to apologize for?" he asked.

She smiled at that.

"Agreed. And now I will bring you something to eat." She stood. "What would you like?"

"Anything you recommend."

"I will bring coffee first," she told him, and went to the kitchen.

Chapter Eleven

By the time she returned with coffee, and then with the food, the other diners had paid their bill and left. She sat with him while he ate.

"What have you been doing?" she asked.

"I talked with Lucinda, and then with her husband."

"Carlos spoke to you?" she said. "He is a very jealous husband."

"I know," he said. "I found that out."

"And it is odd, because he is always with some woman," she said.

"He sees other women?"

"Oh, yes."

"Like his secretary?"

"You met Ayesha?"

"Yes," he said, "when I went to his office."

"Why did you go to his office?"

He explained to her about the portrait, and about asking Carlos' permission for his wife to paint it.

"And he said yes?"

"He said we had his blessing."

"That is . . .very strange."

"That's what Lucinda said."

Norina put her chin in her hand and leaned on the table.

"Are you in love with her, yet?" she asked.

"What? No."

"She is closer to your age," she said.

"That has nothing to do with it," he said. "I told you before, she's married. I'm just going to let her paint me."

"Will you pay her?"

"Of course."

"That might be why Carlos agreed."

"He's a lawyer," Clint said. "Doesn't he do well?"

"He is one of the wealthiest people in town," she said. "But he does not give Lucinda any money. She must earn her own."

"But she's his wife."

"It does not matter," she said. "A woman must earn her own money."

"Does your father pay you for your work?"

"Yes," she said, "but not very much. Still, I am saving."

"For anything special?"

"Yes," she said. "I am saving to leave Santa Fe."

"And go where?"

"Just away from here," she said. "Away from my father."

"Before you leave," he advised her, "you should have a destination in mind. Think about it. It could even be somewhere close, like Albuquerque."

"I'll think about it."

"Tell me more about Carlos," Clint said.

"He is not a good man, or a nice man," she said. "I would be very careful of him if I was you. He will not trust you with Lucinda. Many men have fallen in love with her, only to disappear."

"Disappear?"

"Or they were killed."

"By Carlos?"

"I do not think he does his own killing," she said. "He has . . . friends."

"Friends who kill for him?"

"If he tells them to."

"Those don't sound like friends," Clint said.

"They are bad men."

"Do you know them?"

"I know one," she said. "A man named Barrett. He is not Mexican, but he is always with men who are."

"Carlos is sounding more and more dangerous than just a jealous husband," Clint said.

"That is what I am telling you, Clint," she said. Be very, very careful."

Chapter Twelve

When Clint left Norina, he felt he knew enough about Carlos Montalban to be wary of him. In fact, it was enough for him to cancel his portrait sitting and just leave town. But he was far from the kind of man who would run, and if he left, that was what he would be doing. So, he felt he had no choice but to honor his commitment to Lucinda, while watching her husband very carefully.

He also wondered what he could find out about a man called Barrett? He decided he might as well make a visit to the local law and see what they could tell him.

During one of his walks around town he had spotted the sheriff's office, so he walked there and entered. There was a man seated behind a desk in a small office. He saw the flash of a badge on the man's shirt, but it was partially blocked by a vest, so he couldn't tell if he was the sheriff, or a deputy. Given his age, though, he assumed a man in his forties would be the sheriff.

"Sheriff?"

"That's right," the man said. "Sheriff Al Cody. And you are?"

"Clint Adams."

"The Gunsmith," Cody said. "When did you get to town?"

"A couple of days ago."

"That's odd," Cody said. "I usually hear of the arrival of men with reputations."

"I did my best to keep it quiet."

"So why come to see me now?"

"To avoid trouble."

"Are you after somebody," the lawman said, "or are they after you?"

"Neither one," Clint said. "Starting tomorrow I'll be getting my portrait painted."

"By who?"

"An artist named Lucinda."

"Carlos Montalban's wife?" Cody asked. "Does he know about this?"

"He does," Clint said. "In fact, he gave us his blessing."

"Now that doesn't sound like the Carlos I know," Cody said.

"That's what I'm here to find out," Clint said. "What do you know about him?"

"I know he's jealous as hell," Cody said.

"I heard he's killed some men out of jealousy."

"One that we know of," Cody said. "Others have . . ." He paused.

". . . disappeared?"

"Yes."

"And what about a man named Barrett?"

"Hank Barrett," Cody said, frowning at the mention of the name. "What about him?"

"I heard he does things for Carlos."

Now Cody sat up straighter.

"Who've you been talkin' to?"

"That doesn't matter, does it?"

"Hank Barrett is pretty much muscle for hire," Cody said. "And he often hires out to Carlos."

"Carlos is a lawyer," Clint said. "What's he need muscle for?"

"Well, sometimes clients don't pay him on time," Cody said. "Sometimes clients don't like the outcome of their cases, so Carlos needs protection."

"And is Barrett a hired gun?"

"No," Cody said, shaking his head emphatically, "strictly muscle. Oh, he wears a gun, but he'd much rather use a knife, or his hands."

"And does he have men who work with him?"

"A few," Cody said. "It depends on the difficulty of the job."

"And you're all okay with all this?" Clint asked.

Cody bristled.

"I do my job, Adams," he said, "when I have to."

"Of course," Clint said. "Sorry, I didn't mean to offend you."

50

"Look," Cody said, "if all you're gonna do is have your picture painted by Lucinda, then you shouldn't have any trouble."

"I just wanted to check in."

"I have to ask," Cody said. "Is there anythin' else goin' on between you and Lucinda?"

"Not a thing," Clint said. "She's just going to paint my portrait. And it's a paying job."

"And what will you be wearin' while she's paintin' you?" Cody asked.

"Everything," Clint said, "including my gun."

"Well," the lawman said, "try not to use it while you're in town."

"I'll do my best," Clint said. "Believe me, I don't use my gun unless I have to—no matter what you've heard."

"Okay, then," Cody said. "Thanks for stoppin' by."

"No problem."

Clint left the sheriff's office, wondering if he had just had a conversation with one of Carlos Montalban's friends?

Chapter Thirteen

Clint decided to stop in a saloon for a beer. Maybe he would hear something interesting, or a bartender might know even more than the sheriff did.

The first saloon he came to had a sign over the door that read simply THE CACTUS. As he entered a few patrons looked up at him, but then went back to their drinking and talking. It was a small saloon and he could clearly see the clientele was local. He didn't see any guns.

He went to the bar, where a tall, young bartender asked, "Can I get you somethin'?"

"Beer."

"Comin' up."

As the bartender set the beer in front of him he said, "You're not local."

"What gave me away?"

The bartender smiled.

"I haven't seen you before."

"And you know everybody in Santa Fe, do you?" Clint asked him.

"I know a lot of the people, yes," the man said. "At least, the ones who drink."

"Well, that's good," Clint said. "Maybe you can help me, then."

"If I can."

"I'm about to have my portrait painted by one of your local artists."

"Which one?"

"Her name's Lucinda."

"Hey, she's a very good artist," the man said. "You picked a good one."

"Do you know her?"

"I know of her," the man said. "By the way, my name's Daniel. What's yours?"

"Clint. Do you know of her husband?"

"Ah, Carlos," Daniel said. "Yes, he's been in here once or twice. I do know him."

"And do you know his friends?"

"I understand he has lots of friends," Daniel said. "He's a very popular man who, I believe, will soon run for mayor of Santa Fe."

"Ah, I didn't know that," Clint said. "So he wants to be a politician."

"Oh, yes."

"That explains a lot."

"And just what is it you're tryin' to find out?" Daniel asked.

"I'm just wondering about the kind of man I'm dealing with," Clint said. "And I don't know when I'm talking to a good friend of his, or not. For instance, I spoke to the sheriff earlier today, but I don't know if he and Carlos are close friends."

"I see. Are you wonderin' if I'm friends with Carlos Montalban?"

"I am."

"I'm not," he said. "And there are no friends of his in here."

"How can you be sure?"

"These men are all local merchants who have had dealing with Montalban as a lawyer. It was never pleasant. They don't like him."

"And you?"

"I told you he was in here a couple of times," Daniel said. "What I didn't tell you is that he never drank when he was here. In fact, he sneered at the very idea of actually having a drink here."

"Then what was he doing here?"

"He wanted to buy my place."

"Ah," Clint said, "but you didn't want to sell."

"No, I didn't."

"How did he take it?"

"He came back with some of his friends, to try to convince me."

"And what happened?"

"I introduced him to a friend of mine." With that Daniel brought a double-barrel shotgun out from beneath the bar and set it on the surface.

"Ah, that friend," Clint said. "And how did they react to that?"

"Well." Daniel said, "they haven't been back."

"How long ago was this?"

"Last month."

"Why do you think he wants this place?"

"I can only assume he'd tear it down and build something else here. He's already bought the properties on either side of me."

"Then you're probably right," Clint said. "And, if he's bought other places on this street, he's probably not going to give up."

"I'll be ready." He put the shotgun back under the bar.

Clint finished his beer and paid for it. But before leaving he had another question.

"These friends that Carlos brought with them," he said. "Was one of them named Barrett?"

"Yes," Daniel said, "he called one of them that. A big man, as tall as me but much heavier."

"What part did he take in the conversation?"

"He wanted to use force to convince me," Daniel said. "Carlos stopped him."

"So he does what Carlos tells him?"

"That's how it looked."

"Okay, thanks, Daniel. You've been very helpful."

"You're welcome," Daniel said. "Come back again for a drink."

"I will," Clint said, "if you're still here." He started for the door, then stopped and turned. "By the way, if you need my help for any reason, let me know."

"I will," Daniel said, "if you think you can really help, but I need to know what hotel you're in, and your full name in order to find you."

"I'm at the Cathedral Hotel," Clint said, "and my name's Clint Adams."

He left without waiting to see if Daniel recognized his name.

Chapter Fourteen

Clint appeared at the La Dama Artistica gallery the next morning, following breakfast in his hotel. He was greeted by a young man, who stood behind the counter.

"I'm Jack," he said. "Lucinda is waitin' for you in her studio."

"Thanks."

He found Lucinda doing something to a canvas she had set on an easel. She was wearing a long, white apron to protect her dress from paint spatter.

"Good morning," he said.

"Ah, good-morning, Mr. Adams."

"Clint, please," he said. "I mean, you are about to paint me."

"I am preparing the easel to accept my paints, Clint," she told him. "I'll only be a few minutes. Meanwhile . . . I like the new shirt. A very vivid blue."

"I know," he said. "I cheated by buying it, but—"

"It is fine," she said. "If I did not like the color, I could change it, but I do like it."

"Good," he said. "Then it was money well spent."

"There," she said, "my easel is ready, as are my paints. Now, we need only to get you ready."

"Oh, I'm ready."

"No," she said, "you're willing. We have to work on your pose in order to get you ready."

He was surprised that she worked with him for a good hour just to get the right pose.

"I had no idea this part was so important," he said, at one point.

"Point your elbow a little more . . . yes, it's very important . . . bend your knees slightly . . . and you'll have to be in this pose each day."

"That shouldn't be hard," he said. "After one day I'll probably be stuck in it."

"There," she said, stepping back, "I think we finally have it."

She went to her easel to observe him from there.

"Good," he said, "I was starting to get tired—"

"No," she said, cutting him off, "not yet." She came back around the easel. "Chin up," she said, putting her hand beneath his chin.

What had he gotten himself into?

On the other hand, it was no chore working so closely with a beautiful woman who was intent on touching him all the time. Norina had been right, Lucinda was closer to his age. In fact, she was older than he was, but if she hadn't been married that would have been no obstacle. He had the feeling Lucinda would be beautiful when she was seventy.

"There," she said, finally.

"We've got it?" he asked.

She looked at him from her easel, smiled and said, "We have it." She picked up a brush. "Now we will begin."

***

After two hours, she put her brush down and asked, "Are you hungry?"

"Starved," he said.

"Why don't you go and have something to eat, and then come back," she suggested.

"I can move?"

She smiled.

"You can move but remember where you were."

He relaxed.

"Why don't you come with me to eat?" he asked.

"I have some food here," she said. "I will be fine. Come back in one hour."

"All right," he said. "I'll see you then."

He started to leave the studio, but then stopped and turned.

"By the way," he asked, "who's Jack?"

"Just someone I use to sit in the gallery when I am back here."

"Not a relative? Cousin?"

"No, nothing like that," she said. "I will be paying him out of the money you pay me for the portrait."

"Oh, that's right," he said. "We haven't agreed on a price."

"That is up to you," she said. "It was your idea to pay me."

"So you'll take whatever I want to give you?" he asked.

"I am sure you will be fair."

He considered that, nodded and said, "I'll give it some thought."

***

From a room on the second floor of a building across the street, Hank Barrett watched as the Gunsmith left the building.

Barrett's job, given to him by Carlos Montalban, was to observe the Gunsmith, and Lucinda, while she was painting his portrait.

Knowing the kind of woman, and artist, Lucinda was, he knew she wasn't done, so he knew all he had to do was wait for Clint Adams to come back.

Chapter Fifteen

For the next few days it went the same way. Pose for hours on end, break to go and have a meal. Usually, he went to Norina's café and ate with her. Other times, he just ate at the hotel.

On the fourth day when Lucinda broke for lunch, Clint decided to be a little more forceful.

"What do you eat here when I go to lunch?" he asked.

"Oh, usually fruit, some vegetables."

"Well, today you're coming with me."

"Thank you, but no," she said. "I have some things—"

"Never mind," he said, taking her hand. "You're going to come with me and have a proper meal. We'll go to Norina's."

"Clint—"

"I'm insisting."

She looked down at her hand in his, and then said, "All right."

They left the studio together, but before they entered the gallery where Jack could see them, she slid her hand out of his. He understood.

"We'll be back in an hour, Jack," she said.

"Enjoy your lunch," he said, waving a hand in which he was holding a sandwich.

They went out the front door.

***

Barrett sat up straight.

This was different.

Over the past few days, Adams left the gallery, went and had some lunch somewhere, and then came back. Lucinda stayed inside. Today, they were leaving together.

He hurried from the room and down a flight of outside stairs, not wanting to lose sight of them.

***

Clint and Lucinda walked directly to Norina's café, where the younger woman greeted them with a puzzled smile.

"Welcome," she said. "You are having lunch together today?"

"It is not my idea," Lucinda said. "Clint insisted."

"She doesn't allow talking during the sitting," Clint complained. "This way maybe I'll get to know her a little better."

Norina gave Clint a look, and he knew what she was thinking. But he was not falling in love with Lucinda. He just wanted to talk to her.

"Take any table," Norina said. "As you see, you are my only customers."

Clint took Lucinda to his usual table and they sat.

"Do you always sit in the back?" she asked.

"Yes," he said, "I always like to have my back to the wall when I can. Or, in this case, my side. And I like to be able to see the entire room."

"And this is because of who you are?" she asked. "I mean, the Gunsmith."

"Yes."

"And when someone knocks on your hotel room door?"

"I answer with my gun in my hand."

"That is such a sad way to live."

"For me," Clint said, "it's the only way I can assure that I will go on living."

"Sad," she said, again.

Norina came to the table with a pot of coffee and two cups.

"What may I get you?"

"Enchiladas," Lucinda said. "*Por favor*."

"I'll have the same," Clint said.

As Norina went back to the kitchen, Lucinda said, "I love enchiladas."

"Then why don't you eat them more?"

63

"A woman my age must watch what she eats," she said, "and how often she eats it."

"You look fine to me," he said. "Beautiful, in fact."

"Gracias," she said, "but you should have seen me when I was Norina's age."

"I'm sure you're just as beautiful now as you were then."

"And you are very gallant," she said, "but just look closely at her when she comes out. Her skin, her hair, her eyes . . . she is a vision, as I once was."

"Then maybe she should look at you," Clint said, "to see what she will someday become."

Lucinda laughed.

"And why would we want to depress that lovely young woman?" she asked.

"Lucinda," he said, "doesn't your husband tell you that you're beautiful?"

"Oh no," she said, "he tells me I am lazy, silly, foolish, and that I don't make enough money. That is about all."

"Then why do you stay with him?"

"Because," she said, "if I tried to leave him, he would kill me."

Chapter Sixteen

Norina brought them each an empty plate, and then put a platter of enchiladas in the center of the table. Next she brought plates of rice, beans and lettuce.

"Do you know a man named Barrett?" he asked Lucinda, while they ate.

"Yes," she said. "That is, my husband knows him."

"How?"

"He uses him for . . . certain jobs."

"Jobs that require muscle?"

Lucinda hesitated, chewed and swallowed, then said, "Yes."

"Then why is Barrett following us?" he asked.

She froze.

"What?"

"He's been watching your gallery ever since we started the portrait," Clint said. "He's never followed me when I left for lunch. But he followed us today."

She put down her fork.

"I don't know," she said, "but I can guess."

"So can I," Clint said. "Your husband wants to know what we're doing."

"I tell Carlos every night what we have been doing," she said.

"Then he's got Barrett confirming that you're telling him the truth."

She pushed her plate away.

"I have suddenly lost my appetite," she said. "Let's go back to the gallery."

He looked down at his plate. He was just about finished, anyway.

"Okay."

Norina came out of the kitchen and asked, "You are finished?"

"Yes," he said. "We have to get back."

He paid the bill, then he and Lucinda left the café.

"Where is he?" she asked, as they got outside.

"For a big man, he knows how to stay out of sight," Clint said. "But he'll follow us back."

"Then let's go," she said, and started walking briskly back toward the gallery.

***

Back in the studio Lucinda prowled the room, obviously angry.

"He gave us his blessing," she said. "That's what you said."

"That's what *he* said," Clint corrected.

"And where is that man Barrett now?" she asked. "Where is he watching us from?"

"A window in a building across the street."

"A building my husband owns," she said. "He bought it and forced the people there out of business. It is now empty."

"Except for the man named Hank Barrett," Clint told her. "What else does he do for your husband, Lucinda?"

She remained silent, facing one of the white walls with her arms folded.

"Has he killed for him?"

She turned to look at Clint. She still had her arms folded, and now she began to massage her upper arms, as if she was very cold.

"Why would my husband need to have Barrett kill?" she asked. "Kill who?"

"Someone he thought was your lover," Clint said. "Somebody who wouldn't sell their business to him?"

"If my husband thought I had a lover, he would kill the man himself."

"And a business rival?" Clint asked. "Or political rival?"

She closed her eyes and shook her head.

"He's a cruel man, in business and at home, but murder . . ." She shook her head, again.

"But you believe that he'd kill you if you left."

"Yes."

"Wouldn't that be murder?"

"He would not see it as murder, Clint," she said. "He would see it as his right."

"Well," Clint said, "I can't agree with that."

She turned away from him again, staring at the wall. He thought she might be feeling something akin to guilt.

"Why don't we quit for today?" she said. "Thank you for taking me to lunch."

"Lucinda—"

"Please," she said, "I have a headache. I can't paint when I have a headache."

"All right," Clint said. "Tomorrow."

He walked through the gallery and left without saying a word to Jack, who just watched.

***

Barrett was surprised when Clint Adams came out of the gallery so soon. He decided not to follow him, assuming he would be coming back for the sitting.

Two hours later he knew he was wrong . . .

Chapter Seventeen

Clint knew he should simply sit for his portrait and stay out of Lucinda and Carlos' marriage, and the man's business, but none of this sat right with him.

He decided to go back to the Cactus Saloon and talk with Daniel, the bartender and owner. Maybe talking to him about Carlos Montalban might help to make up his mind to either step in, or stay out of their business.

"Welcome back," Daniel said, as Clint entered the empty saloon.

"Tough crowd," Clint said, approaching the bar.

"It's early," Daniel said. "In a couple of hours you'll see two, maybe three people in here. Regulars."

"Ah."

"Beer?"

"Please."

Daniel set it down in front of him.

"You here for more talk?" Daniel asked.

"What makes you say that?"

"You don't look especially thirsty."

"Well then, yeah, I came to talk," Clint said, "and to drink."

"Why don't we sit down, then?" Daniel suggested. "I mean, since nobody else's here."

"Suits me."

Daniel drew himself a beer, then followed Clint to a table against the back wall.

"You can see everything from here," the bartender said.

"That's the idea."

"So, what's on your mind?"

"Still Carlos Montalban," Clint said, "and his man, Barrett."

"What about them?"

"Seems he's bought up a bunch of buildings in Santa Fe, and emptied them out."

"That's so he can knock 'em down eventually, and build himself something else."

"Like what?"

"Don't know, yet," Daniel said. "He ain't started buildin'. Maybe a saloon."

"Do you know if he's used Barrett for any killings?" Clint asked.

"I couldn't tell you that," Daniel said. "But I know he was ready to kill me, if Montalban gave him the word."

Clint rubbed his jaw, thoughtfully.

"He's got Barrett watching me and Lucinda. He even followed us to lunch today."

"You had lunch with her?" Daniel asked. "In a restaurant?"

"Yep."

"Barrett's gonna tell Montalban about that," Daniel said, "and he ain't gonna like it."

"Probably not."

"He'll probably give her a whippin'."

"I wouldn't like that," Clint said.

"Would you kill him?"

"Not if I didn't have to."

"And Barrett? Wouldja kill him?"

"Only if he forced my hand," Clint said.

"Well," Daniel said, "I doubt either one of them would face you head on. You better be on the lookout for a bullet in the back."

"Lucinda said if Carlos was jealous of a man, he'd kill him himself."

"I'm sure he would," the bartender said, standing up, "if the man wasn't the Gunsmith."

As Daniel walked back to the bar with their two empty glasses, Clint thought he probably had a point.

Chapter Eighteen

Convinced that Clint Adams wasn't going to return to the gallery, Barrett knew he had to go and tell Carlos Montalban.

He walked to the lawyer's office and entered. The girl sitting at the desk looked up at him with fear in her eyes that she tried to hide. He liked having women be afraid of him, but today he didn't have time to play with her.

"Is he in?"

"Uh, y-yes, he is."

"Good."

"You can't just go—" she said, but he marched past her and entered Montalban's office.

The lawyer looked up from some papers he was reading and frowned.

"What are you doing here?" he asked. "You are supposed to be watching the gallery."

"I was," Barrett said. "Adams left the gallery about two hours ago, and he never came back."

"Why did he do that?"

"I don't know."

Montalban frowned.

"Why would they quit early?"

"I don't know."

"Is my wife still there?"

"She was when I left," Barrett said. "At least, she didn't use the front door."

Montalban stood up.

"I'm going over there and find out."

"Do you want me to come with you?"

"No," Montalban said. "I think I can handle my wife myself. But see if you can locate Adams, and find out what he's doing."

"All right."

They left the office together after Montalban told his girl he would be back shortly. Outside they went in their own directions.

***

Clint noticed that Barrett hadn't followed him to the Cactus. The man probably thought he'd be coming back to the gallery for his portrait, not knowing they had quit early for the day. He wondered how long the man would wait before giving up? And would he then inform Montalban?

He decided to go and see for himself.

***

When he entered Montalban's office, the girl, Ayesha, looked up at him from her desk.

"Is Mr. Montalban in his office?"

"He's not," she said. "He went out."

"Who with?"

She made a face. "That man, Barrett."

"You don't like Barrett?"

"I'm afraid of him," she said. "He knows it, and he likes it, and that makes me also hate him. But he works for Mr. Montalban, so . . ." She shrugged.

"Where'd they go?" he asked.

"I don't know," she said. "They rushed out, and Mr. Montalban told me he would be back shortly."

"Thank you."

He turned to leave.

"Are you going to try to find him?"

"I am."

"Be careful of Barrett," she said, "He's a brutal man."

"Thanks for the warning," he said. "I'll keep it in mind."

"And if you get the chance." she said.

"What?"

"Kill him."

***

When Clint got to the gallery, the front door was locked. He peered in the window, but didn't see anyone— not Lucinda, not Montalban, and not Jack. He wasn't sure whether or not this was a bad sign. Why would the gallery be locked this early in the day?

He decided to go around the back and see if he could get in that way. There was no door leading to the studio, but he did see a back door to the storeroom.

He circled the building, got to the back and tried the door. It was locked, and very solid. Next, he walked to the window of the studio and looked in. He couldn't see the whole room, but he saw the easel, and the place where he had been posing. There was no sign of Lucinda.

He tried the window, found it locked tightly. The situation was not an emergency, so he didn't feel justified in breaking it to enter.

He returned to the back of the building, where there were windows leading to the storeroom. He could have broken one of them to get in, but when he reached down to see if he could pry it, it opened easily. He climbed through, walked through the storeroom to the studio, hoping he wouldn't find Lucinda there in a corner he couldn't see from the window.

He didn't.

She wasn't there, but her husband, Carlos was.

He was in a corner, propped up against the wall, and he was dead.

Chapter Nineteen

Clint walked to the body and bent over it. Carlos Montalban had been shot in the chest. From the amount of blood on the floor around him, he must have bled out.

He looked around the studio and found everything was in place. There was no evidence that any kind of struggle had taken place. Had he come in, threatened his wife, and been shot by her? Where would she have gotten a gun? Did he have one with him? And if so, how did she get it?

He went back to the body and did a quick search. There was nothing of any help. The man's skin still felt warm, so he had been killed a short time ago.

Finding that back window unlocked had been a surprise. Maybe now he knew why. Whoever had killed Montalban had left by way of that window—and maybe had gotten in the same way. But what was Montalban doing here, and why wasn't Lucinda around?

Clint realized he needed to get out of there, and report this to the sheriff. The lawman might think he had killed the lawyer, but he thought he could talk him out of that.

He left the studio, went through the storeroom to the window, and climbed out. He wanted to keep things the way they were when he entered.

"Hold it right there, Adams!"

He froze, turned his head and saw the sheriff standing there, holding a gun on him.

"Sheriff," he said, "I know this must look odd—"

"You climbing out the window of a locked gallery?" the sheriff asked. "What's odd about that?"

"Sheriff—"

"I think we better get Miss Lucinda to open up her gallery and see if anythin's missin'."

"Do I look like I have anything on me?" Clint asked.

"Then what are you doin' here?"

"I was worried about Lucinda," Clint said.

"Why?"

"When I came back, the place was locked up," Clint said. "That's not right."

"So you let yourself in?"

"I thought she might be in trouble."

"And?"

"And she's not here."

"Then what'd you find?"

"Okay," Clint said, "don't overreact to what I'm about to tell you."

Cody frowned.

"What?"

"Carlos Montalban is inside," Clint said, "and he's dead."

Al Cody had looked as if he was going to holster his weapon, but now he brought it up and pointed it at Clint again.

"Did you kill 'im?"

"No, I didn't."

"Well," Cody said, "let's go inside and have a look."

"The back door's locked," Clint said. "We'll have to use this window."

"Which you forced?"

"I didn't have to," Clint said. "It was unlocked."

"Okay, here's what we're gonna do," Cody said. "You're gonna climb in and open the back door for me. If you try to get away—"

"You can lean in and keep me covered, Sheriff," Clint said. "I'm not going anywhere."

"Then let's do it."

***

When Clint unlocked the back door and opened it, Cody pointed his gun at him, again.

"You don't need that," Clint told him.

"Before we go any further," Cody said, "I'm gonna need your gun."

"I can't do that," Clint said. "Not unless you arrest me."

"I don't have anythin' to arrest you for, right now," Cody said. "Not if your story is true."

"Then I suggest you holster your gun, and come and have a look."

Cody thought it over, then holstered his weapon.

"Where is he, the studio?"

"Yes,"

Cody walked to the studio without waiting for Clint to show him the way.

"Jesus," he said, when he saw Carlos Montalban sitting in a pool of blood.

Clint was actually glad the lawyer was still there. He had the most uncomfortable feeling that the body would be gone.

Cody went and bent over the body.

"One shot to the chest," he said.

"Yes."

The lawman turned and looked at Clint. He seemed to be very saddened by the fact that he had holstered his gun. Now he was unsure whether or not to try to draw it again.

"I didn't kill him," Clint said.

"How do I know that?"

"If I had, why would I have come back here, climbed in a window, and climbed out again after I found him?"

"What if you didn't," Cody said. "What if I just caught you climbing out after you killed him?"

"Well," Clint said, "you're just going to have to decide what you believe, Sheriff. And if you think I killed him, you're going to draw your gun, right?"

"Against you?" Cody said. "That'd be suicide."

"I didn't kill him," Clint said, "and I'm not going to kill you."

Cody hesitated, then said, "Okay, then maybe I should just get the doctor over here, and then we'll go and see Lucinda. Maybe she can shed some light on all this."

"That's a good idea," Clint said, but as they left the gallery by the back door, he kept his eye on the lawman, in case he decided to try for his gun.

Chapter Twenty

The doctor's name was Silas Taylor, and he immediately left his office and returned to the gallery with Clint and Sheriff Cody. Others in town, seeing the sheriff and the doctor, naturally assumed something was wrong, and followed.

When they reached La Dama Artistica, Cody went in the back door and then opened the front for the doctor. He allowed Taylor and Clint to precede him, then turned to the crowd and said, "Nothin' to see here. Go home!"

But nobody moved, so he simply went inside.

The doctor examined the body, then stood and turned to Clint and the sheriff.

"I don't know what you want me to tell you, Al," he said. The men must have known each other a long time, were about the same age, and called each other by their first names. "He ain't been dead that long. I think he bled out."

"Okay, Silas," Cody said. "Can you arrange to get him over to the undertaker's?"

"Sure thing," Taylor said. "There's enough of a crowd out front for me to get four men to carry the body over."

"Good."

"What about his wife?" Taylor asked. "Does she know?"

"Not yet," Cody said. "We're gonna go over and tell 'er."

"If she ain't already heard from some nosy citizen," Taylor said.

As the doctor went out to get help, Cody turned to Clint.

"Tell me what happened here today."

Clint told Cody about sitting for his portrait that morning, going to lunch with Lucinda, and then returning to the gallery.

"And she kept workin'?"

"No," Clint said, "she said she had a headache and had to stop."

"What gave her a headache?"

"It might have been the fact that I told her Montalban had a man watching us."

"So he didn't trust you two?"

"I guess not."

"Was anything goin' on besides paintin'?" Cody asked.

"Not a thing, sheriff."

"Who was the man watchin' you?"

"Barrett."

"Oh," Cody said. "He usually has Barrett do more than just watch."

"Maybe that was the plan."

"Did you actually see Barrett?"

"Every day," Clint said. "Usually he'd follow me to lunch and back, then watch until we quit. Today he followed both of us to lunch."

"And when you left, did he follow you?"

"No," Clint said. "I thought maybe he waited a while, then went and told Montalban that Lucinda and I had lunch together."

"He wouldn't have liked that."

"I know it. The more I thought about it, the more worried I got. That's why I came back."

"What did you think he was gonna do?"

"Sheriff, it seems to be public knowledge that he hit her," Clint said. "And she told me that if she ever tried to leave, he'd kill her."

"But instead, he got killed."

Clint nodded. The doctor returned with four men, who lifted the body and carried it out.

"Do you think she killed him?" Cody asked.

"It's not likely," Clint said. "I never saw her have a gun in here. Did Montalban carry a gun?"

"Not usually," the sheriff said. "He left that to Barrett."

"Then maybe you should find Barrett."

"I know my job, Adams," Cody said. "By all rights I should toss you in a cell."

"What for?"

"Safekeeping."

"From what?"

"When the word gets around that Carlos was shot to death, who do you think folks are gonna suspect?"

***

Al Cody led Clint to what looked like the most expensive house in town. It was two floors, with white columns in front.

They went to the front door and Cody knocked. Clint wondered if a servant was going to answer, but when the door opened it was Lucinda standing there.

"Clint," she said, surprised. "And Sheriff Cody. What can I do for you?"

"I think maybe you better come with us Ma'am," Cody said.

"What for?"

"Somethin's happened at your gallery."

"Did somebody break in?" she asked, alarmed. "Was there damage?"

Clint and the sheriff had agreed that it would be Cody who told her about her husband.

"I'm sorry, Lucinda," Sheriff Cody said, "but Carlos is dead."

"What? How?"

"Somebody shot him."

Lucinda immediately looked at Clint.

"Not by me," he said.

"Where did it happen?" she asked.

"In your studio."

"What was he doing there?"

"We don't know," Cody said.

"What about Ayesha? Does she know?"

"I haven't had a chance to talk to her yet," Cody said. "I wanted to tell you . . ."

"Thank you, Sheriff," she said. "Where is . . . he, now?"

"At the undertakers."

"Then I should get over there."

"Do you want me to go with you?" Clint asked.

She looked at him again for a moment before speaking. At that time, he knew she was thinking he might have killed Carlos.

"No, thank you," she said. "I will be fine. You go with the sheriff."

"Right."

"Thank you both. I should get dressed."

She was wearing a dress, but Clint assumed this meant she wanted them to leave.

"We'll talk again later," Daly said. "I'll need to ask you some more questions."

"Yes, all right."

She closed the door. Daly turned to Clint.

"She thinks you did it," he said. "A lot of people will."

"Let's see what we can find out from his girl, Ayesha," Clint said. "And later, you question Lucinda some more."

"Yes, fine."

They started walking back to town.

"We should also find Barrett."

"You think his own man killed him?" Daly asked. "Why would he?"

"Maybe they had a falling out."

"Montalban was payin' him," Daly sad. "Why would they have a fallin' out?"

"Could be Carlos wanted Barrett to do something he didn't want to do."

"I don't think there's anythin' Barrett wouldn't do," Daly said.

"I still think it would be worth talking to him," Clint said. "Maybe he knows something."

"Okay," Daly said, "but Carlos' girl, first."

"Agreed."

Chapter Twenty-One

When they walked into Carlos Montalban's office Ayesha looked up from her desk.

"Where is he?" she asked.

"He's dead, Ayesha," Clint said. "Somebody shot him."

She put both hands over her mouth, then dropped them to her lap.

"Who did it?" she asked Cody. "Was it Barrett?"

"Why would you think it was Barrett?" Cody asked.

"Because he's a brutal, horrible man," she said.

"Well," Cody said, "we don't know who did. That's what I'm gonna have to find out. Do you know anybody else who might wanna kill 'im?"

She looked at Clint.

"Other than Mr. Adams."

"Not offhand," she said.

"Well, could you give it some thought?" Cody asked. "There must be a few people he did business with who might've wanted him dead."

"Okay," she said, "I will."

"Let me know if you come up with anythin'," Cody said.

"Do I have to stay here?" she asked.

"No," Cody said, "you can lock up and go home."

"Thank you."

They turned to leave.

"Uh, where was he killed?" she asked.

"In Lucinda's studio," Cody said.

"Well, then," Ayesha said, "maybe she did it."

"Just keep thinking about it," Clint said.

"Yes, all right."

They left the office.

Outside Cody said, "I don't know if she's gonna be much help."

"She already gave you three suspects," Clint said.

"Yeah, but they were three I already had," Cody said.

"So what are you going to do next?" Clint asked.

"I don't know," the sheriff said. "I'm not a detective."

"But you must have had people killed in town before?" Clint said.

"Sure, but it's always been real obvious who did it," Cody said. "Drunks, husbands, wives, gunmen . . . but I've never dealt with this before."

"You mean murder?"

"Right."

"Well," Clint said, "so far you're going about it the right way. Just ask questions."

"Right."

"Meanwhile," Clint said, "I better see Lucinda."

"She's not sure you're innocent," Cody said.

"I know," Clint said. "I have to convince her that I am."

"Well," Cody said, "maybe you can also convince me."

Clint stopped walking and turned to look at Cody, who also stopped.

"For now," Cody said, "I'm just gonna assume you didn't kill Montalban."

"Thank you," Clint said, "but I get the feeling if you thought you could get your gun out faster than I could, I'd be in jail right now."

"We'll never know, will we?" Cody asked. "Because I ain't about to try."

"Good," Clint said, "don't."

"I'm goin' to go to my office now," Cody said. "I need time to think."

"I'm going to go find Lucinda," Clint said. "I'll see you later."

"Do I need to tell you not to leave town?" Cody asked.

"No," Clint said. "You don't."

They each nodded, turned and went their separate ways.

Chapter Twenty-Two

As Clint entered the undertaker's office, a man turned to look at him.

"Sir?" he asked. "Are you bereaved?"

If Clint didn't know better, he might have thought the man was an actor. He had a smooth, handsome face and broad shoulders. A sign over his door said his name was Abraham Bishop. He should have been on stage.

"No, I'm not," Clint said. "I'm here looking for Lucinda."

"Ah," Bishop said, "she's with her husband now, in the back. Would you like to join her?"

"No," Clint said, "I'll wait for her here."

"Very well."

Bishop went back to doing whatever he had been doing when Clint entered. Clint simply stood there and waited. He hoped when Lucinda came out, she wouldn't look at him the way she had at her house.

It took about fifteen minutes, but she finally came from the back, saw Clint and smiled.

"I am so glad you're here," she said. "We should go back to the studio and continue." She looked at the undertaker. "Thank you, Abraham."

"You're welcome, Lucinda," he said. "And I'm very sorry."

She took Clint's arm and guided him outside.

"Lucinda," he said, as they started walking, "are you sure you want to keep painting my portrait?"

"More than ever," she said. "Carlos is gone now."

"Yes," Clint said. "He's dead."

"Of course," she said. "I know that. You killed him. And I thank you."

"Lucinda," he said, "I didn't kill your husband."

"No," she said, "of course not."

"Really," Clint said. "I didn't. I just went to the studio and found him there."

"Why did you go there?"

"I was worried about you."

"Well, now you need not worry anymore," she said. "He's dead. He can't hurt me, anymore."

"No, he can't."

"Thanks to you."

He stopped walking. She continued for a few feet then stopped. People walked around them and stared.

"Lucinda—" he said.

"I know." She grinned. "You didn't kill him."

She turned and continued walking.

***

When they reached her gallery, they stopped in front.

"I have to warn you," he said. "There's a lot of blood on your floor."

"That's all right," she said. "I will clean it."

She unlocked the door and went inside. They walked through the gallery, the storeroom, to the door of the studio. On the floor where he had found Carlos was a circle of blood with a space inside where he had been sitting.

"He was sitting with his back to the wall," Clint said.

"I see," she said. She looked around. "There is no damage."

"No," Clint said. "Apparently, there was no fight of any kind. Somebody just walked in and shot him."

She looked at him. He knew what she was thinking.

"I keep telling you—"

"I know," she said, touching his arm. "You did not kill him." She walked into the room, stood just outside the circle of blood. "You should go. I will clean up, and we will begin again tomorrow."

"All right."

He turned to leave. He was almost to the front door when she came from the back.

"No, wait."

He turned.

"Come to my house tonight for supper," she said. "I will cook."

"Lucinda—"

"Please."

He hesitated, then nodded and said, "All right."

Chapter Twenty-Three

Clint walked back to his hotel.

Along the way people stopped and stared. He could only assume the word had gone around town that Montalban was dead. As the sheriff had assumed, people thought he had done it.

When he got to his hotel, he went to his room and stayed there until it was time to go to Lucinda's house for supper. He had second thoughts about it, but didn't want to leave her waiting, so he locked his door and walked to the house. Along the way he was treated to more looks from the locals.

When he got there he knocked, and Lucinda answered. She was wearing a dress that hugged her figure rather than hid it. It was now obvious that she had the voluptuous body he had always suspected.

"You're just in time," she said. "Come in."

He entered and followed her into a plushly furnished living room. From there he could see a table set for supper.

"I'm getting suspicious looks from everyone in town," he told her.

"I know," she said. "I stopped at the mercantile for some groceries, and people were talking. But they do not know how happy I am that Carlos is dead. And how grateful I am."

"Grateful?"

"I know," she said, "you say you did not kill him . . ."

"Well," he said, "why should you think differently from anyone else."

"Sit," she said. "I will bring the food."

She went to the kitchen and he sat at the table to wait. He realized, as the aromas came from the kitchen, that he was hungry. He only hoped she could cook as well as she painted.

They talked while they ate.

Actually, she talked and he mostly listened. She told him of the life she thought she could now lead without Carlos holding her down. The things that she thought she could do.

"He even controlled what I would wear," she said. "But as you see . . ."

"I do see," he said. "You should never wear anything that hides you from view."

"I will not, from now on," she said.

"Have you heard from the sheriff?"

"Yes, he came by to ask some questions. Mostly, if I thought of anyone who would want Carlos dead."

"And you said?"

"I gave him many, many names," she said. "He should not be thinking about you, any longer."

He studied her. She had probably given Cody as many names as she could, thinking she was protecting Clint. She obviously still thought he had killed Carlos, no matter how much he denied it.

As it turned out, she was an excellent cook, evidenced by the succulent hunk of beef she had prepared, along with vegetables and biscuits.

"This is Carlos' wine," she said, as they also drank. "He would never let me have any."

"It's very good."

"I do not like it," she said. "But it is expensive, and he would hate that we are drinking it."

"In that case," he said, holding out his glass, "more please."

***

They finished their supper and she cleaned the table off, then returned with coffee and a pie.

"Did you bake this?" he asked.

"I did not have time," she said. "I bought it from a cafe."

"Norina's?"

"No," she said. "I did not want her to know you were coming here."

"Why not?"

"She is young," she said. "She would have been jealous."

"There's nothing to be jealous of."

"You have not lain with her?"

"No."

"Why not?" she asked. "It is obvious she wants you."

"As you say," Clint replied, "she's very young."

That answer seemed to satisfy her.

After the coffee and pie—an excellent apple—she said, "Sit on the sofa. I will finish cleaning."

He nodded, went to the sofa and sat. He heard her in the kitchen, and then she returned and sat next to him.

"Did you get the . . . uh, did you clean your studio?" he asked.

"Oh, yes," she said. "When we continue tomorrow, there will be no sign of Carlos' blood."

He nodded.

"And you're sure you want to keep painting?"

"Yes," she said. "Painting is the one thing I did on my own, and not because Carlos made me."

"It's good that you've always had that."

"Yes, it is."

She moved closer to him, and before he could say anything or react, she leaned in and kissed him.

"That is also something I do because I want to," she whispered.

And he found that he wanted to, as well.

Chapter Twenty-Four

When Ayesha opened the door, Hank Barrett glared at her.

"What do you want?" she demanded.

"I wanna come in."

"What for?"

"We gotta talk."

"About what?"

"You know what," he said. "Your boss. My boss. Our boss."

"He's dead," she said, rubbing her upper arms like she was cold. Barrett still scared her, even knowing she could control him if she wanted to, if she allowed him into her bedroom.

"Ayesha," he said, "I gotta come in."

"To my home?"

"I won't break anythin'," Barrett said. "I promise."

She took a deep breath, let it out in a long sigh, and said, "All right, come in."

As Barrett entered the small house and closed the door, she walked to a dresser drawer, opened it and took out a small gun. When she turned, she pointed it at the brutish man.

"Now what's that for?"

"You scare me, Barrett."

He grinned.

"I know, but I ain't here to scare you," he said. "Put it away."

"I think I'll hold onto it for a while," she said. "What do you want?"

"I need a place to stay."

"Why?"

"I don't wanna talk to the law."

"Why not?"

"Me and the law, we don't get along."

"Did you kill Carlos?"

"Wha—no! Why would I kill 'im? He was payin' me real good money."

"Who do you think killed him?"

"Probably the Gunsmith," Barrett said. "Over his wife."

"You don't think Lucinda could've killed him?" she asked.

"Why would his wife kill 'im?"

"Because she hated him," Ayesha said. "He used to beat her, humiliate her, control her—"

"She was his wife," Barrett said. "He had the right to do those things."

"You're crazy," she said.

"Look," he said, "I just need a place to stay."

"Well, you can't stay here."

"Why not?"

"I told you," she said "you scare me. Also, the sheriff will want to talk to me, so he's going to come here."

He scowled.

"Yeah, you're right about that," he said. "What if I just stay the night?"

"Barrett—"

He started to undo his belt.

"You could make me feel better."

She cocked the hammer on the little gun.

"Those days are gone, Barrett," she said.

"Yeah, I know," he said. "You were with Mr. Montalban. But he's dead now. You're gonna need somebody else."

"Not you!"

He frowned.

"I was good enough for ya once."

"I'm older now," she said. "You scare me, but not as much as you used to."

"You liked it," he said. "I know you did."

"Time for you to go, Hank," she said. "Find someplace else to hide."

"You're a mean girl, Ayesha."

"I told you," she said, "I'm older now. I'm not that young girl you used to rape."

"That what you call it?"

"That's what it was."

He turned, put his hand on the doorknob, then turned back.

"Do me a favor."

"What?"

"Keep your mouth shut about that to the sheriff."

"Don't worry, I don't want anybody to know about it," she told him.

"Good."

He opened the door and left. Ayesha rushed to close and lock it. Then she walked to the dresser and put the gun away.

***

Barrett walked away from the house, shaking his head. He thought he could get the girl to do what he wanted, but she had changed. He never expected her to have a gun.

When he heard his boss was dead, he figured the Gunsmith did it, but he also knew the sheriff would want to talk to him. And he didn't want to talk to the law.

He didn't want to leave Santa Fe, either. He liked it there, but he needed someplace to hide until everything blew over.

Or maybe if he put a bullet into the Gunsmith, that might end it.

Chapter Twenty-Five

"Whoa," Clint said, holding Lucinda at arm's length for a moment.

"What is it?" she asked. "I thought you liked me?"

"I like you a lot," he said. "But your husband just died."

"I know," she said. "That is why I want to take you to bed with me. If we had done it while he was alive, he would have killed me. And tried to kill you."

"But now he's the one who's dead."

"Yes."

"And that makes you happy?"

"I told you," she said. "He used to beat me. If I tried to leave him, he would have killed me. But now . . ."

"Now it's different."

"Very different," she said. "I have my life back again, and I can do what I want with it."

She stood up, reached behind her to undo something, and her dress fell to the floor. Beneath it she was naked. Her breasts were large with heavy undersides, and large brown nipples. Between her legs was a furry thatch as black as the hair on her head.

"And right now, this is what I want to do."

She took his hands and, with surprising strength, pulled him to his feet. She pressed her hot body against him, put her arms around his neck and kissed him. His body reacted, and he kissed her back, sliding his hands up and down her back.

"Now," she said, drawing her head back, "do you want to talk, or come with me to the bedroom."

"Oh," he said, "the bedroom, by all means."

She smiled, took his hands again, and led him there . . .

***

Sheriff Al Cody sat in his office, trying to figure out his next move. If he hadn't been such a coward, he'd have the Gunsmith in a cell, right now. He'd had a meeting with the mayor, and the man told him his job depended on finding out who killed Carlos Montalban, because the lawyer was an important man in Santa Fe.

"And if it turns out to be the Gunsmith," Mayor Havestock told him, "you better take care of him."

"I'll need some deputies, then."

"You'll have 'em," the mayor said. "As many as you need. You just pick 'em out."

Now he was trying to figure out just who he could hire as deputies. Who would take the job, realizing they would eventually have to go up against the Gunsmith?

Then he thought of Barrett. If he could find the man, then maybe . . .

***

In the bedroom Lucinda slowly undressed Clint, after he set his gunbelt close by. When she had him naked, she stared at him, then reached down and took his hard cock in her hands.

"Wonderful!" she said, stroking it.

He ran his hands over her body at the same time, feeling the same way. She had a womanly body, full and curvy, probably as perfect as it could be, even though she was in her mid-forties.

She fell to her knees and pressed his penis to her face, enjoying the smooth feel of it, the heat . . . and then she licked it until it was good and wet. Once that was done, she opened her mouth and took it inside. Clint gasped, reached down to hold her head as it bobbed back and forth. Her full lips glided over him as she cupped his testicles in her hands, gently.

When he thought he couldn't hold out any longer, that her hot, avid mouth was bringing him to the brink, he reached down and pulled her up and pushed her down on the bed . . .

***

"Stop right there, Barrett," Sheriff Al Cody said.

Barrett stopped and put his hands up

Cody had been right. Barrett went to Carlos Montalban's girl, Ayesha. For what? Help?

"What were you doin' here?" Cody asked.

"Just visitin' a friend, Sheriff," Barrett said, turning around.

"Did you know your boss was dead before you came here?" the lawman asked.

"Yeah, I heard," Barrett said. "The Gunsmith killed him."

"Is that a guess?"

"Maybe," Barrett said, "but a good one. Him and Lucinda . . . well, they was doin' more than paintin'."

"And you told that to Montalban?"

"I told 'im what I saw," Barrett said. "That's what he was payin' me to do."

"And what did he do then?"

"He headed for the gallery."

Cody thought a moment, then holstered his gun.

"Okay, look," he said, "I'm gonna need help takin' the Gunsmith in. I got a deputy's badge for you, if you want it."

"Me? A lawman?"

"You wanna be a lawman? Or a suspect?"

"Well," Barrett said, "if those are my choices, I guess I'll take the badge."

"Good," Cody said, "now we're gonna need a few more men. Do you know anybody?"

Barrett grinned.

"I got a few fellas in mind, yeah."

Chapter Twenty-Six

When he had Lucinda on her back, he explored her entire body with his hands and his mouth. He kept at her until she was gasping and writhing beneath him, his face pressed to her wet pussy, his tongue driving her to gushing.

When her body had been wracked by pleasure at least three times, he removed his mouth, kissed his way up her body, to her full breasts and hard nipples. While sucking them he pressed the head of his cock to her loins and pushed, entering her cleanly. She gasped and brought her legs up, wrapping them around his waist.

"As many times as my husband raped me," she gasped, "it was never like this."

"Was it always rape?" he asked.

"Not in the beginning," she said. "At the start we gave each other pleasure, but it soon changed. He started taking his pleasure elsewhere, and with me it was just . . ."

". . . rape," he said.

"Yes."

He kissed her, moved in and out of her as she grunted and gasped.

"This," she said, "oh my God, this . . . is . . . paradise!"

***

The saloon was called The Bloody Bucket. Cody knew it well, but rarely went there, except during his rounds. And even then he didn't go inside, just peered over the batwing doors, and moved on.

Now, however, he followed Barrett in. There were men at the bar, and at tables, two girls working the floor, and they all turned to look.

"Holy Jesus," one man cried out, "is that a badge on your shirt, Barrett?"

"It is," Barrett said, as he and Cody went up to the bar.

"And that's Sheriff Cody," someone else said. "Howdy, Sheriff. What brings you here tonight?"

"Yeah," someone else said, "you usually peek in over the doors and run."

They all laughed at that, the men and the women. Cody knew he had to do something, so he drew his gun and fired it into the air.

"Shut up, all of you!" he bawled. "I'm here on official business."

"Does that mean you won't have a beer?" the bartender asked.

"Two beers, Lew," Barrett said. Then he turned his back to the bar. "I want you boys to listen to what the sheriff has to say. Got it? Anybody who don't listen will hafta answer to me." He looked at Cody. "Go ahead."

"Carlos Montalban was murdered today," Cody said. "It's up to me to bring the guilty party in."

"Well, he ain't in here," somebody yelled.

"Besides," another voice called, "we heard the Gunsmith done it."

"And if he did, I've gotta bring him in," Cody said. "For that I need deputies."

"Is that why yer wearin' a badge, Hank?" somebody asked.

"That's it," Barrett said. "Montalban was an important man in this town. Some of you did jobs for him, like I did. Now he's dead, and we can't let that go."

"Yeah," another voice said, "but the Gunsmith?"

"He's just a man," Cody said, "and with enough men, I can bring him in."

"I told the sheriff he'd find such men here," Barrett said. "Don't make a liar outta me, boys."

"And what do we get for it?" a voice asked.

"You get to be one of the men who took down the Gunsmith," Barrett said. "The legend. And what happens when you bring down a legend?"

"You become a legend!" somebody shouted.

113

They all cheered.

"I've got badges right here," Cody said, dropping them on the bar. "Who wants one?"

He and Barrett waited.

***

"Wait, wait, wait . . ." Lucinda gasped.

"What?" he asked.

"I want to turn around."

He withdrew his cock from her hot depths, watched as she rolled over, got on all fours, and presented her majestic butt to him.

"Get back in there," she said.

He got on his knees behind her, held her hips, slid his penis up between her heavy thighs and plunged into her, again. Then he began to fuck her, driving into her, at the same time holding her hips and pulling her to him. The bed began to jump as they both grunted with the effort. The room filled with the scent of fucking, a mixture of perspiration and fluids. And they both surrendered to it all . . .

Chapter Twenty-Seven

Lucinda turned onto her side and draped a leg over Clint, who was lying on his back. At the same time, she slid her hand down and took his semi-hard cock in her hand.

"You see?" she said. "My husband being dead is very good for both of us."

"I have to admit," he said, "that was good. But you do know that I didn't kill him, right?"

"You keep saying that."

"Because it's true."

"Then if it wasn't you," she asked, "who was it?"

"Well," Clint said, "the sheriff was wondering if it was you."

"Me?" she asked. "I couldn't have killed him."

"Why not?"

"I feared him," she said. "If I tried to kill him and failed, he would have killed me."

"Then who do you think might've killed him, other than me?" he asked.

"Anyone whose business he destroyed," she said. "Anyone whose wife he slept with. Any politician whose career he destroyed."

"So, a lot of people."

"Yes."

"I don't think I'm going to be able to leave Santa Fe until I find out who did it."

She closed her hand around him and squeezed.

"That does not sound like bad news to me," she said.

Before he could comment, she slid onto him, covered him with her body, and took him inside. Once he was completely engulfed, she sat up and began to ride him. Her breathing started to come faster, matching his, and then she leaned forward, reached out and took hold of the bed post, which caused her pendulous breasts to dandle in his face. They were like ripe fruits he could not resist tasting. When he bit her nipples, she gasped and moved her hips faster and faster. He stayed with her as long as he could, impressed that she exhibited more stamina than many younger women he had been with. Finally, her insides seemed to simply yank his ejaculation from him. He tensed, and then bellowed as he exploded inside of her.

***

"That was loud," she said, later.

"Sorry."

They were lying side-by-side, the sweat drying on their bodies, regaining their breath.

"Do not apologize," she said. "It was a most honest response to what we were both feeling."

"I agree with that."

"And now we must sleep, and rest," she said. "You will stay the night, and sleep with me?"

Since there was no chance of her husband returning and finding them together, he said, "I don't see why not."

She nestled into him, her head on his shoulder, and said, "And in the morning we can bathe and breakfast together."

In moments, her breathing told him she was asleep.

***

In the morning Sheriff Cody was waiting in his office for his new deputies. He knew they were men he might have, at one time, tossed into a jail cell, but now he was going to have to use them.

There was still no more solid a suspect in Carlos Montalban's murder than Clint Adams—at least, according to the mayor. Havestock wanted Cody to bring Adams in, and hold him for trial. Cody hated to do it, but he thought that while Adams was in a cell, he could continue to look for other possibilities.

His office door opened and Hank Barrett walked in. He looked like he had bought a new shirt to pin his deputy badge on.

"'mornin'," Barrett said, then added, "sir."

"Good-mornin', deputy," Cody said. "Where are the others?"

"They'll be along," Barrett said. "They were kind of celebratin' last night."

"Celebratin'?" Cody asked. "You mean, drinkin'?"

"Well, yeah, but don't worry, Sheriff," Barrett said. "They'll be here."

"They better be," Cody said. "I wanna find Adams this mornin' and get him into a cell."

"You think you can do that?" Barrett asked.

"I think we can," Cody said. "When he sees how many men we have, he'll give up his gun."

"And if he doesn't?" Barrett asked. "Do we kill 'im?"

"Only if he gives us no other choice," Cody said. "Do you understand that?"

"Sure."

"This is not like the jobs Carlos Montalban used to give you, Barrett," Cody said.

"I know that," Barrett said.

"Okay, well, make sure the others know it, too," Cody told him.

"I will."

The door opened at that point and three men entered, all wearing deputy badges.

"Good-mornin'," Cody said, "here's what we're gonna do . . ."

Chapter Twenty-Eight

Clint woke briefly when Lucinda got out of bed.

"Stay where you are," she whispered to him. "I will come and get you when breakfast is ready."

Clint drifted off to sleep again, but woke when he heard Lucinda come back into the room. She leaned over, kissed him, and said, "Breakfast."

He got out of bed and stood there a moment, naked.

"I brought you a robe. It was my husband's." She handed it to him. "Don't worry, it's been laundered."

"Thank you."

He put the robe on. Montalban was taller than him, so the sleeves were a little long, and the hem hung down to his ankles, but did not touch the floor.

Downstairs he found the table laden with eggs, bacon, potatoes, and tortillas. As she sat, she poured him a cup of hot coffee.

"I thought we deserved a hearty breakfast, after last night," she said.

"I agree."

She sat across from him and they both ate voraciously.

"And after this we could take a bath together," she said.

"You know what that would lead to, Lucinda."

She smiled.

"Yes, I do."

"I'll have to forgo it, then," he said. "I need to get out there and find out who killed Carlos."

"Because you are in a hurry to leave town?" she asked.

"No," he said, "because I don't want people—and you—looking at me like I did it."

"If you say you did not kill him," she said, "I believe you."

"Good," he said, "now I just need to make everyone else believe it, too."

***

When they finished eating breakfast, he went upstairs and got dressed, then came back down. She was still seated at the table, where he had told her to wait. He knew if she went up with him, they wouldn't come down for quite a while.

"What are you going to do today?" he asked.

"I will make arrangements for Carlos' burial," she said. "Then I will go to the studio to keep working on your portrait."

"And you can do that without me?"

121

She smiled.

"You are burned into my memory, Clint."

"Then I'll come and see you later at the gallery," he said.

"I will be waiting."

He first opened the door and peered out. He didn't want anyone to see him leaving. Knowing that he spent the night with the widow would only strengthen people's opinion that he killed Montalban. When he was sure no one was around, he left.

***

Sheriff Al Cody took his new deputies with him to the hotel to see if Clint Adams was there.

"I don't know if he's in his room, Sheriff," the clerk said. "I can only tell you I didn't see him come down."

"All right." Cody turned to his new deputies. "Let's go up and check. And remember, no gunplay unless it's absolutely necessary."

"We've got it, Sheriff," Barrett said.

They went upstairs and knocked on the door of Clint Adams' room.

"Maybe he just ain't answerin'," Barrett said.

"Why not?" Cody asked. "He doesn't know we're comin'. In fact, he doesn't know I hired special deputies.

He's got no reason not to answer the door, if he's in there."

"We could kick it in and check," one of the men offered.

"No," Cody said, "we'll just keep lookin' for him. Maybe he's havin' breakfast, somewhere. Come on."

They went back down to the lobby, and out onto the street.

***

Clint was approaching the hotel when he saw Sheriff Cody come out with four men who were wearing badges. One of them was a hulking giant of a man, he could only guess was Barrett. He ducked into a doorway so they wouldn't see him.

He watched as they stopped on the boardwalk in front of the hotel, talked for a bit, and then the four men followed Cody down the street.

Clint assumed that Cody had hired the deputies to back his play when he tried to take him in. Now he was going to have to try to avoid them while he was looking for Montalban's killer. And he had to also assume he was doing that alone.

Once the "lawmen" had disappeared down the street, he stepped out of the doorway and entered the hotel.

"Mr. Adams!" the clerk said, surprised. "I thought you were upstairs, sir."

"I saw the law leaving," Clint said. "They were looking for me, weren't they?"

"I'm afraid they were, sir."

"And the big one," Clint said, "was his name Barrett?"

"I believe it was."

Further proof that Cody meant to arrest him for the murder. He must have been convinced that Barrett didn't do it, and decided to hire the man as a deputy. The other deputies had to be the same kind of men. Cody meant to bring him in, or kill him.

He needed to catch Cody alone to find out the lawman's reasoning.

Saddling Eclipse and getting out of town was not an option. He couldn't ride around with a price on his head for murder, and that was probably what would occur if he left. No, he had to stay and not only prove his innocence, but find out who really killed Carlos Montalban.

"Um, will you be keeping your room, sir?" the desk clerk asked.

"Yes," Clint said, "for a while." He took out some money and handed it to the young man.

"What's this for, Mr. Adams?"

"If the sheriff comes back, or his deputies, don't tell them you saw me, and there'll be more."

The clerk looked at the money in his hand, then tucked it into his pocket and said, "Whatever you say, sir."

Chapter Twenty-Nine

Clint had to get Sheriff Cody alone, without his new deputies. He had to convince the lawman not to try to arrest him. The chaos that would cause would be too great a price to pay.

The sheriff and his rented lawmen would probably be looking for him elsewhere. That meant they would go to the La Dama Artistica gallery next.

He headed there.

***

Jack came to the doorway of Lucinda's studio and said, "The sheriff's here."

"What does he want?" she asked.

"He wanted to know if Clint Adams was here," Jack said. "I told him no. Then he asked for you. Should I tell him you went out the back?"

"No," Lucinda said, putting down her brush. "I'll talk to him."

She went out front with Jack, found Al Cody there with four other men wearing badges.

"Sheriff," she said.

"Mrs. Montalban," he said. "Can we talk?"

"We can if you have your . . . deputies wait outside," she said. "I can't have bulls in my china shop, if you get my meaning."

"Who she callin' a bull," Barrett complained.

"She means you boys are too big to be in here," Cody said. "There's no room. Wait outside."

Still mumbling about being called a bull, Barrett went out with the others.

"What can I do for you, Sheriff?" Lucinda asked.

"I'm sorry to bother you while you're in mournin'," Cody said, "but I'm lookin' for Clint Adams. I thought he was here—you know, for his portrait."

"He was, but he's not here, right now."

"And he's not at his hotel," Cody said. "Would you know where else he might be?"

"I'm afraid I have no idea," she said.

"Well," the lawman said, "if you should see 'im, would you tell 'im I'm lookin' for him. I just . . . need to talk."

"With four deputies?"

"They're new," Cody said. "I was just . . . showin' them around."

"I see. Very well, I'll tell him."

She watched as Cody went out the front door.

"They're not new," Jack said.

"What?"

"That big one, I've seen him in town before. A couple of the others, as well."

"I thought so," she said. "The big one was Barrett. He worked for my husband."

"Right."

"So they probably came here to do more than just talk to Mr. Adams," she said.

"I agree."

"Well, Jack," she said. "Keep an eye out for him."

"Yes, Ma'am."

Lucinda went back to her studio.

"Are they gone?" Clint asked.

***

As Clint approached the gallery, he saw Sheriff Cody and the four deputies go in. He waited until the door closed behind them, then went around to the back. The rear door was unlocked, so he went in, heard the voices from the gallery, and went to wait in the studio. That's where he was when Lucinda came back in.

"Are they gone?" he asked.

She was startled, but then smiled at him.

"Yes, they're gone."

"Did they say what they wanted?"

"Yes," she said. "Sheriff Cody said he wanted to talk to you."

"So he brought four deputies with him?"

"That's what Jack and I said."

"Jack's here?"

"Yes, why?"

"I want to talk to Sheriff Cody, but I need to get him alone," Clint said. "Can you send Jack to get him?"

"I'll tell him," she said. "You wait here."

"Wait," he said, as she started to leave. "We need to give him a reason to come alone."

"I will give Jack one," she said. "Leave it to me."

"Yeah, but—"

"Mr. Adams," she said, "do you think I do not know how to get a man to come and see me?"

"Uh, no," he said, "I don't have any doubt at all about that."

Chapter Thirty

"Sheriff!"

Cody turned and saw the young man from the gallery coming toward him. Barrett and the other deputies also turned.

"I'm glad I caught you," Jack said.

"What is it?"

"Mrs. Montalban thought of somethin' she should've told you," he said. "She'd like you to come back to the gallery."

"All right," Cody said, and to the deputies, "let's go."

"No," Jack said, "she wants you to come alone."

"Why?"

"She also told me not to come back with you," Jack went on. "She, uh, wants to be alone with you."

Cody stared at the young man for a few moments. She was a new widow, and he happened to know that she and her husband didn't get along. Now that he was gone . . .

"All right," Cody said. "You fellas go back to my office and wait. I'll be there . . . soon."

"Right," Barrett said.

He led the men toward the office, while Cody and Jack went back toward the gallery.

***

"Will you kill him when he gets here?" Lucinda asked.

"Why would I do that?"

"He is going to try to kill you, isn't he?"

"I hope not."

"Then why did he come here with four deputies?" she asked.

"Probably to arrest me, put me in a cell."

"Arrest you for what?"

"For killing Carlos."

He had decided to go ahead and pose for her while they were waiting for jack to come back with Cody. Now she looked up from her easel.

"But you said you did not kill him."

"I didn't," Clint said, "and Cody can't figure out who did. He's probably getting pressure to make an arrest. So I'm the logical choice."

"What are you going to do to him, then?"

"Try to convince him to change his logic," Clint said.

***

As Jack and Cody approached the gallery, Jack said, "You better go on in. I have some other things to do."

"Yeah, sure, kid," Cody said.

Jack ran, ducked in the alley next to the gallery and went around back. The door was unlocked so he ran in, and by the time he got to the studio, he was out of breath.

"He's in the gallery," he gasped.

"Go out and talk to him," Clint said, "and entice him back here. I'll do the rest."

Lucinda nodded, left the studio and went to the gallery. Cody turned as she entered.

"I was just startin' to think the boy was kiddin' me," he said.

"Why?" she asked. "What did he tell you?"

"He said you, uh, wanted to see me . . . alone."

"I do," she said "But not here. Somebody might . . . walk in on us."

"Huh?" Cody said, swallowing hard.

"Please," she said, "come in the back with me." She crooked a finger at him. "This way."

"Oh, uh, sure," he said, and followed.

As he went through the door behind her, he suddenly felt something poke him in the back.

"Just stand still and don't panic, Sheriff," Clint said. He plucked the man's gun from its holster. "We're going to have a little talk."

Chapter Thirty-One

Lucinda locked the back door, then went into the gallery and locked the front.

In the storeroom Clint told the sheriff to have a seat on a crate.

"What are you gonna do?" Cody asked.

"Talk," Clint said, "we're just going to talk. See?" He holstered his gun.

Cody knew that if he made a move the Gunsmith didn't like, he could get that gun right back out again in a split second.

"We are locked," Lucinda said, returning from the front. "Do you need me for anything else?"

"No," Clint said, "you can have a seat, or you can go home."

"I will be in my studio, working on your portrait," she said, and left.

When she was gone Cody asked, "What's this all about? You know my deputies are gonna come here lookin' for me."

"You really expect them to be that smart?" Clint asked. "They're going to stay right where they are until getting the word from you."

"Are they gonna hear from me?"

"Well, sure, what do you think?"

"I think you're gonna kill me."

"Look, Sheriff," Clint said, "I didn't kill Carlos, and I'm not going to kill you."

"Then why am I here?"

"You're here because I don't want you trying to arrest me," Clint said.

"What makes you think I'd do that?"

"You hired four deputies," Clint said. "And look who you hired. The big one's Barrett, right?"

"Right."

"What makes you think he didn't kill Carlos?"

"He says he didn't."

"Well, for Goddssake," Clint said, "I say I didn't and you're ready to come after me."

"Look," Cody said, "I'm under a lot of pressure from the mayor. He says Carlos was an important man in this town, and we can't let somebody get away with killin' him."

"So then you might as well arrest me."

"If I have you in a cell," Cody said, "the pressure's off, and then I can go out and find who really did it."

"Wouldn't it be better if we went out and found the killer together?"

Cody took a deep breath and let it out slowly.

"I don't think I could get the mayor to go for that," he said.

"Well then," Clint said, "maybe I should go and talk to the mayor."

"You can do that." Cody stood up. "Let me know what happens. Now can I have my gun—"

"No."

"No?"

"No, I mean, I want to talk to the mayor now," Clint said. "Take me over to his office and introduce me."

"Wha—now?"

Clint stood.

"Right now."

"I-I don't even know if he's in his office."

"Well," Clint said, "if he's not, we'll go to his house."

"We can't—"

"Yes, we can," Clint said. "Let's go."

"What about my gun?"

Clint took the gun from his belt, cracked it open, ejected the shells, closed it and handed it to the sheriff.

"Now let's go."

He told Lucinda they were leaving, and he would see her later.

***

They had almost reached the City Hall building when Clint asked, "Have you ever thought about the mayor?"

"Thought about him how?" Cody asked.

"You know, that maybe he killed Carlos," Clint said. "Or had him killed."

"Why would the mayor have him killed?"

"I don't know," Clint said. "Politics? Maybe he thinks Carlos was going to run against him, at some point. I understand he's new to the job."

"So?"

"So maybe he wants to make sure he keeps it for a long time," Clint suggested.

"That's crazy."

"Is it?" Clint said. "He's known Carlos for a while, right?"

"Yeah."

"So it makes more sense to you that I, who only just met him, would have a reason to kill him? But not somebody who's known him for a while?"

"By that logic, there're a lot of people in town who might wanna kill 'im."

"Thank you!"

Chapter Thirty-Two

As they approached City Hall, a new looking, two-story brick building, Clint asked, "Is that his window?" pointing up as they entered.

"No."

"Really? Most of these guys like to look down on their domain."

"Not him," Cody said. "He likes to sit in the back of the building."

"What do you know about that," Clint said. "I might end up liking this guy."

Cody doubted it.

They went up to the second floor and walked to a door that had MAYOR'S OFFICE written on it. As they entered a bespectacled, granny looking woman with grey hair looked up at them.

"Sheriff," she said, "you don't have an appointment."

"I know, Mrs. Havestock. This is Clint Adams. He'd like to see the mayor."

"Is that right?" She looked at Clint. "And do you have an appointment?"

"No," Clint said, "but I'd like to make one."

"Very well." She opened a book. "When?"

"Now," he said, and walked past her.

"Hey, you can't—" she started, but he was already through the door into the mayor's office.

A man rose from behind a large desk and stared at Clint.

"What the hell—"

"Are you the mayor?" Clint asked.

"That's right," the man said. "Mayor Havestock."

"Well, listen—Havestock?"

Clint looked at the grey-haired woman who had come in and was standing next to him.

"I couldn't stop him," she said.

"It's all right, mother," the mayor said. "I'll talk with Mr. Adams."

She nodded, backed out and closed the door. It didn't escape Clint's notice that the sheriff was gone.

"So," Mayor Havestock said, "the famous Gunsmith." He stared at Clint officiously, but since he was not yet forty, Clint didn't take him all that seriously.

"Forget that," Clint said. "Your sheriff is probably going to be back here any minute with those phony deputies you let him hire."

"I assure you—"

"Never mind," Clint said. "I need you to stop pressuring the sheriff to arrest me."

"And why would I do that?"

"Because I didn't kill Carlos Montalban."

"And am I supposed to take your word for that?" Havestock asked.

"No," Clint said, "but when I find out who did it, then you can take my word for it."

"And what makes you think I've been pressuring the sheriff?" the mayor asked.

"Why else would he hire four deputies?" Clint asked. "And men like Barrett, who probably belong behind bars, not behind a badge."

"I'm sure the sheriff knows how to do his job," the mayor said.

"All right, let's put it this way," Clint said. "I'm telling you that I'm going to find out who killed Carlos Montalban. I want you and the sheriff to stay out of my way."

"Are you threatening us?"

"Let's say I'm advising you."

"And what would you do, Mr. Adams?" Havestock asked. "Kill us?"

"Only if you leave me no other choice."

Suddenly, the mayor didn't look so officious.

"You'd, uh, kill me?"

"If you make me," Clint said.

"But . . . I don't carry a gun."

"And I don't kill unarmed men."

"Well," Havestock said, "that's good—"

"Not usually, anyway," Clint said. "But you might force me into making an exception."

"Um, and how would I do that?"

"I'll give you a for instance," Clint said. "If I leave this office and the sheriff is out there with his deputies, there's going to be trouble. And once I finish with them, I'll come in here and take care of you."

"Finish with them?" Havestock asked. "You believe you can handle five men?"

"You said I was famous, Mr. Mayor," Clint said. "What do you think I'm famous for?"

Havestock sat back in his chair and cleared his throat.

"What would you have me do?"

"I think," Clint said, "when I leave your office, you better come with me. Then you can tell the sheriff the agreement we've come to."

"And exactly what agreement have we come to?" the mayor asked.

"I'll tell you . . ."

Chapter Thirty-Three

When Clint opened the door of the mayor's office to leave, he found himself looking at five guns. Cody and his deputies quickly extended their arms, pointing their guns at the Gunsmith.

"That's far enough, Mr. Adams," Cody said. "Let me have your gun."

"Can't do that, Sheriff."

"You're gonna have to," Cody said.

"I don't think so."

The mayor came out behind him.

"Put your guns up, boys," he said.

"Mayor? What the—"

"Mr. Adams and I have come to an agreement," Mayor Havestock said. "Send your men away, Sheriff, and come inside. We'll talk about it."

"Mr. Mayor," Cody said, "we've got 'im."

"Put your gun away before he kills you, Sheriff," Havestock said. "And you boys, out of my office. Now!"

The deputies looked at each other, then holstered their guns and left.

"Inside, Al," the mayor said.

The sheriff holstered his gun and, puzzled, entered the mayor's office. Havestock looked at Clint, then followed and closed the door.

The mayor's mother gave Clint a dirty look.

"What did you do to him?" she demanded.

"I just got him to give me a little time," Clint said. "Maybe you can help me, Mrs. Havestock."

"Oh? How?"

"How well did you know Carlos Montalban."

She hesitated a moment, considering the question, then said, "I knew Carlos' father, and his mother. And I knew him when he was a boy. But as a man? I didn't know him, at all. And I didn't want to."

"Why not?"

"Because he was a horrible man," she said. "He went from a sweet young boy to a horrible man. He used to beat Lucinda, you know."

"I do know."

"So maybe you'd better look at her, if you're looking for someone who wanted him dead."

"She's on my list," he said. "Who else should be on it?"

"Not my son!" she snapped. "Now, if you please, I have work to do."

"I just have one more question."

***

Clint knocked on the door and waited. It was opened by Ayesha, Carlos Montalban's secretary. His last question to Mrs. Havestock had been whether or not she knew where Ayesha lived. She did. Apparently, she knew where everyone in Santa Fe lived.

"Mr. Adams," she said.

"Good, you remember me."

"Of course," she said. "Come in."

He entered, closing the door behind him. It was a small house, well cared for on the outside. The inside seemed well-furnished, but messy, at that moment. There were items of clothing scattered about.

"Excuse the mess," she said. "I've been trying to find another job, and I need different clothes for different interviews."

"I see."

She stopped in the middle of the room and turned to face him.

"What can I do for you?" the pretty young woman asked.

"Tell me about your boss."

"My former boss?"

"Yes," Clint said, "the dead one."

"He was a lawyer," she said, "but he did a lot more than practice law."

"That's the kind of thing I want to know."

"Do you?" she asked. "Bad enough to buy me supper?"

"And dessert," he said. "You pick the place."

She smiled and said, "Let's go."

***

Ayesha led him to an expensive looking restaurant with gold paint on the windows saying it was EL GATO LOCO STEAK HOUSE.

"El Gato Loco?" he said. "The Crazy Cat?"

"Weird name," she said. "Great food."

They went inside and were seated at a quiet table for two away from the door. The waiter smiled at Ayesha and handed them menus.

"Do you mind?" she asked Clint.

"Go ahead."

"Two pork chop dinners, Arthur."

"As you wish, Miss Ayesha."

As the waiter walked away, Clint asked. "Do you have a last name?"

"I never use it," she said. "Everybody in Santa Fe knows me just as Ayesha."

"And do they all know you worked for Carlos?"

"Why don't you ask me all your questions now, Mr. Adams, so when our food comes, we can just eat?"

Chapter Thirty-Four

"Did you kill him?" Clint asked.

"And put myself out of a job?" she asked. "Why would I do that?"

"I understand he didn't treat women very well."

"He used to beat his wife," she said. "All he ever made me do was pleasure him."

"And you continued to work for him?"

"He paid me very well," she said, "and I happen to like sex. And the answer to your next question is, no, I don't consider myself a whore. I was very good at my job."

"All right," Clint said. "Do you have any idea who killed him?"

"Well," she said, "At first I thought it was you."

"A lot of people seem to think that."

"Then I thought maybe it was Lucinda."

"You don't think that anymore?" he asked.

"Not about you," she said, "but I'm not so sure about Lucinda."

"Anyone else?" Clint asked. "Say, a man named Barrett?"

"He's an animal," she said, "but I don't think he would kill the goose who was laying his golden eggs. He was being paid too well."

"Are you sure?"

"That he was being paid well? Dead sure. I arranged for the payments. But am I sure he didn't kill him? Barrett came to my place and asked me to hide him. He said he didn't kill Carlos, but he didn't want to talk to the sheriff either. I believed him."

"But you didn't hide him?"

"He's always frightened me. I didn't want to be alone with him."

"Can you think of anyone else?"

"Mr. Adams—"

"Just make it Clint."

"Clint," she said, "almost anybody who did business with Mr. Montalban wanted to kill him."

"That's what I keep hearing."

The waiter came and set their plates down, with two mugs of beer.

"Can we eat now?" she asked Clint.

"Sure, let's eat."

***

After supper they walked back to Ayesha's house, and talked along the way.

"So tell me," she asked, "what've you been doing with Lucinda in her studio?"

"Posing."

"That's all?"

"That's it. Did Carlos think different?"

"Well, the day he was killed he ran out, heading for the gallery. It was because of something Barrett told him."

"I don't know what that was."

"And you weren't dallying with her?"

"No."

"Why not? She's beautiful."

"She was a married woman," he said. "I don't dally with married women."

"Well," she said, "that's interesting."

When they got to her house, they stopped at the front door.

"Would you come inside with me, please?"

"Do you have something else to tell me?"

"I don't know where Barrett is," she said. "I'm not sure he won't be in there."

Clint knew where Hank Barrett was, but he didn't tell her. He thought there might still be something he could get out of her.

"All right. But I'll go first."

"Good."

She gave him the key, let him unlock the door and go inside. He found an oil lamp on a table and lit it, then looked around.

"It's clear," he said. "You can come in."

She entered the small house and closed the door.

"How did you manage to afford this house?" he asked her. "If you don't mind me asking."

"I told you," she said. "I'm very good at my job. Carlos bought it for me."

"Did he own it?" Clint asked. "Will you lose it now that he's dead?"

"No," she said, "he put it in my name."

"Ayesha, what about Carlos' relationship with the mayor?" he asked.

Her eyes widened.

"You think the mayor killed him?"

"What do you think of that?" he asked.

"I think it would be more likely for the mayor's mother to kill him."

"Why would she do that?"

"She loves her son," Ayesha said, "and Carlos had no respect for him, at all. She knew that."

"Would she do it herself, or have someone do it for her?" he asked.

"That woman?" Ayesha said. "She might look meek, but believe me, she would do it herself."

"I guess I'll have to talk to her again."

"I'm sure you will," she said, "but not right now."

"How's that?"

"I've had a bad week, Clint," Ayesha said. "I'm still kind of afraid Barrett will come back, and how do I know whoever killed Carlos won't kill me?"

"Why would they do that?"

"We don't know why Carlos was killed," she said. "If it was for something he knew, then I might know it, too."

"I suppose that could be true."

"So what I need is a strong man's arms around me. Can you do that for me?"

"Sure I can."

They took a few steps towards each other and she melted against him as he held her tightly. They stood that way for a while, with the heat from her body and the smell of her hair doing things to him.

"I feel something," she said.

"Ayesha—"

She slid one hand between them and pressed it against the bulge at his crotch.

She drew her head back, smiled, said, "That's what I was hoping it was," and kissed him.

Chapter Thirty-Five

Ayesha was young, but not as young as Norina, the café girl. As she took his hands and drew him to her bedroom, he had no trouble going with her. Once there, her avid mouth attacked his again, and her hands roamed all over him. He ran his hands down her back, found the catches of her dress and undid them. When the garment fell away, he found his arms filled with a naked woman. Her skin was hot and smooth, and her hands went quickly to his belt. He took his gun off, set it within arm's reach, and then he let her do the rest.

She helped him with his boots, removed his trousers, shorts and shirt, and when he was completely naked, she pressed her body to his, trapping his hard cock between them, so she could feel it, hot and throbbing.

She rubbed herself against him, while he ran his hands down to her taut butt and held her by the cheeks. Her hard nipples poked him in the chest.

Then he moved his hands from her butt, took her by the shoulders and held her at arm's length. She was not only tall, but lean, with small breasts and large nipples.

He turned her and pushed her down on the bed. She was like Lucinda, in that she had dark skin and black hair on her head and between her legs. After that the two women differed greatly. But they were both beautiful, and both very willing, two things Clint Adams very much liked in a woman.

He joined her on the bed, started to explore her body with his mouth. The smooth, hot skin, hard, long nipples felt good against his cheeks and lips. She moaned and writhed beneath his manipulation, as he continued to work his way down her abdomen to her belly, where he probed her navel with the tip of his tongue, and then moved on. When he reached the forest of black between her thighs, the scent of her wetness hit his nostrils, his hunger for her increased.

Spreading her legs, he first kissed the tender flesh of her inner thighs, then pressed his face to the mat of black hair, pushing through it with his tongue until he could taste her tartness. She gasped as he avidly licked her up and down, then moved his head side-to-side until she gasped and shivered and screamed . . .

***

He gave her only a few minutes to recover before mounting her a few minutes after and driving his cock into her.

"Oh, yes!" she gasped.

When she wrapped her arms and legs around him, he could feel surprising strength. He had been with Lucinda so recently that he couldn't help but continue to compare the two women. There was not the cushion he had felt while fucking the artist, but Ayesha was hot, smooth and strong, and they had that much in common.

"Oh, God, yes," she said, "harder, Clint . . . do it harder . . ."

So he did it harder, and also faster. While licking her pussy he had been concerned with her pleasure, but while fucking he was concerned with his own. He felt his release building up inside of him, rushing up through his legs and thighs the way lava rushed up a volcano.

"Oh, yes," she said "I can feel it . . . you're going to . . . going to . . . ahhh . . ."

She gasped and bit off a scream when he erupted inside of her. He groaned, and barely kept himself from letting out a loud cry . . .

***

"That was what I needed," she said later, lying beside him. "A strong man."

"So you wanted me to do more than just hold you."

"Oh, yes . . ."

"What about everything else you told me?" Clint asked.

"Oh, that was all true," she said. "I am worried that someone will try to harm me. That's why I've been staying inside all this time, and not looking for another job. And when I stay home, I'm kind of . . . messy."

"I can see that."

She backhanded him on the shoulder, then leaned in and kissed the spot.

"I bet you're going to tell me Lucinda's studio is neat and clean."

"It is," he said. Then he lied. "But I'm not comparing the two of you."

"You couldn't if you wanted to," Ayesha said. "She's too beautiful."

"You're beautiful, too."

"Oh, I know," she said. "Enough of these horrible men in Santa Fe have chased me. But I am not as beautiful as Lucinda. Nobody is."

"I shouldn't argue with you," Clint said, taking her into his arms again, "I'll just show you."

Chapter Thirty-Six

Ayesha reclined on her bed and watched Clint get dressed. She reached out to him.

"I would pull you back into this bed, but you have worn me out," she said. "I need to rest."

"So do I," he said. "You're a very energetic young woman."

She laughed.

"You come back here in the morning, and I'll show you how energetic I can really be."

"If I do that," Clint said, "you might give me a heart attack. And there's still a lot I have to do."

"Like what?"

"Like find out who killed Carlos Montalban."

"Why do you want to do that?" she asked. "What does it matter to you? Why don't you just leave town?"

"I don't want people thinking I did it," he said. "So I can't leave until I find the killer."

"Then I'll help you, if I can," she said, sitting up. He studied her taut body, which showed no indication of the slightest jiggle. She had possibly the smallest breasts, but largest nipples he had ever seen. Lucinda may have had more jiggle and curves to her bountiful body, but Ayesha was no less desirable.

And she was smart.

"I'll take you up on that," he said, "once I figure out how to. Meanwhile, get some sleep and stay inside."

"You'll come back?"

"I'll be back."

He approached the bed, and she reached out again, wrapped her arms around his neck and kissed him.

"Good-night, Ayesha."

"Good-night, Clint," she said, "and thank you . . . for supper."

***

When he left Ayesha's house, he wished he had someone he could put on guard, there. But he didn't even have anyone to watch his own back. He still had no idea whether or not Cody and his deputies would come after him. He had to find this killer and find him—or her—fast.

He went back to his hotel to turn in for the night.

***

In the morning he woke early and went to the hotel's diningroom for breakfast. He decided on a Mexican version, and was rolling his *chorizo*-and-eggs in a tortilla when Sheriff Cody entered.

"Mind if I sit?" Cody asked.

"Have a cup of coffee."

"Thanks."

Cody sat and poured himself a cup from the pot on the table.

"Wow," he said, after a sip, "that's strong."

"The way I like it," Clint said. "What can I do for you, Sheriff?"

"Work with me."

"Really?" Clint asked. "You've given up the idea of arresting me?"

"Well," Cody said, "as long as the mayor says not to. Until then, I think we should work together."

"Do you have any idea who might've killed Carlos?" Clint asked.

"Uh, no."

"Are you prepared to watch my back while we find out?" Clint asked.

"Well, sure. I mean, as long as you don't try to break the law."

"And your special deputies?"

"They've all been . . . fired."

"Were they mad about that?"

"They weren't happy," Cody said, "but they knew it was temporary."

"What about Barrett?"

"Yeah, I took his badge, but I also warned him off you," Cody said.

"Is he convinced you don't think he killed Carlos?"

"Yeah, I think so."

"And you don't?"

Cody hesitated.

"He was on my list, but I had to take him off it when I gave him a badge."

"Well, put him back on it," Clint said. "Ayesha says he's dangerous."

"I know he's dangerous," Cody said.

"What about the mayor's mother?"

"Is she dangerous?" Cody asked. "Yeah, everybody thinks so."

"Dangerous enough to kill Carlos if she thought he was a threat to her son?"

"Wow, is that what you think?"

Clint took a bite of his tortilla, chewed, swallowed and said, "She's on my list."

Chapter Thirty-Seven

"Where are you goin'?" Cody asked, as he and Clint left the hotel.

"To Lucinda's gallery," Clint said. "I want to talk to her again, and I might as well sit for my portrait."

"And what am I supposed to do?"

"Come with me?"

"And do what?"

"Watch my back."

"Watch you while you sit and she paints?"

"No," Clint said, "you can stay outside and watch the door."

"I could do that," Cody said, "but I also have my rounds."

"Okay," Clint said, "while I'm in the gallery, you do your rounds. Then come back."

"Sure, I can do that."

They walked over to the gallery. Sheriff Cody watched Clint enter, then turned and went off to make his rounds.

"Hi, Jack," Clint said, inside. "Is she in her studio?"

"Yes," Jack said. "Go on back, Mr. Adams."

"Thanks."

Clint went back to the studio, stopped and looked at Lucinda, who's back was to him as she worked. He decided to knock so he wouldn't startle her.

"Later, Jack," she said without turning.

"It's not Jack," Clint said.

She turned and smiled. The apron she wore was covered with paint.

"Clint! I'm glad you're here. I need you to sit, just for a short time."

"Good," he said, "I want to talk to you, just for a short time."

"That works out fine, then."

He walked to his place and took up his pose. She asked him to raise his chin a bit, then said, "Perfect. What did you want to talk to me about?"

"The mayor's mother."

"Gertrude?"

"Is that her first name?"

"Yes," she said, "nobody calls her that, but I don't like her, so . . ."

"Why don't you like her?"

"Well, basically because she's a bitch."

"Then let me ask you this," he said. "Is she a bitch who might have killed your husband, or had him killed?"

Lucinda stopped what she was doing and stared at Clint.

"Do you think that's what happened?" she asked.

"I only met the woman briefly," Clint said. "I don't know her, but from what I heard from the sheriff, and some others, she'd do anything for her son."

"That's probably true," Lucinda said, "but I don't know about murder."

"How did she get along with Carlos?"

"He also thought she was a bitch, and he treated her that way. I think she hated him. But still . . ."

"Okay then," Clint said, "come up with another name."

"Like I told you," she said, going back to work on her canvas, "there are a lot of names."

She wasn't being very helpful. Was that because she couldn't, or wouldn't?

He sat for her for about an hour, and then she said she didn't need him, anymore. And since he hadn't gotten much information out of her. He moved to the door to leave.

"I know somebody you should consider," Lucinda said.

"Oh? Who?"

"Ayesha?"

"Really? His secretary?"

"She was much more than his secretary," Lucinda said. "He forced her to . . . do things I'm sure she didn't want to do."

"I'll look into her a bit more, then," he said.

As he left, she was totally engrossed in what she was doing and didn't even look up.

Chapter Thirty-Eight

When Clint got outside, he found the sheriff waiting there, leaning against a post with his arms folded.

"Are you done with your rounds?" he asked.

"Yes. Are you finished with your posin'?"

"I am," Clint said. "I also talked with Lucinda about the mayor's mother."

"What'd she have to say about her?"

"That Carlos thought she was a bitch, and she hated Carlos."

"Well, if she killed everybody who thought she was a bitch, there'd be nobody left in town."

"Maybe we should talk to her," Clint said.

"If I accuse the mayor's mother of killing Montalban," Cody said, "I'm sure to get fired."

"Okay, I'll go and talk to her," Clint said. "Once again, you can wait outside."

"Suits me."

They walked from the gallery over to the City Hall building, and while Clint went inside, Cody once again leaned against a pole with his arms crossed.

Clint went up to the second floor and entered the mayor's office. The mayor's mother looked up at him and frowned.

"He's not in," she said.

"That's fine," he said. "I'm not here to see the mayor, I'm here to see you."

"Me? Whatever for?"

"People have been saying things about you, Mrs. Havestock."

"What kind of things?"

"Oh, that you didn't like Carlos Montalban."

She snorted and said, "Who did? Are you thinking that I might've killed him?"

"Or had him killed."

"Where did you get such an idea?"

"It's been suggested to me by a few people, actually," he lied.

"You mean by that bitch, Lucinda?"

"*She's* a bitch?"

"All women are bitches to each other, Mr. Adams," she said. "I would've thought a man your age would've learned that, by now."

"So do you think Lucinda killed her own husband?"

"If my husband treated me the way he treated her," she said, "I would've killed him."

"So then, you *are* capable of murder?"

"You're going to have to look elsewhere for your culprit, Mr. Adams," she said. "That is, if you, indeed, did not do it, yourself."

"What about your son?"

She glared up at him, and if looks could kill he would have been dead.

"My son is a politician," she said, "and a gentle man. Now you better get out of here before I show you that yes, I *can* kill."

Clint turned and walked out.

***

"How did it go?" Sheriff Cody asked, when he came out.

"Not good," Clint said. "I'm not one of her favorite people."

"So what's next?" Cody asked.

"Let's get a beer and discuss it," Clint suggested.

"We can go across the street—" Cody started, but Clint cut him off.

"No," he said. "The Cactus."

Clint led the way . . .

***

Daniel smiled as Clint entered, then saw Cody behind him.

"Comin' in to close me down, Sheriff?" he asked.

"Two beers, bartender," Cody said. "That's all."

"Comin' up."

While Daniel went for the beer, Clint asked Cody, "Why would he think you were here to close him down?"

"I don't know," Cody said. "You'd have to ask him."

Daniel came back with the beers and set them down. Clint looked around, saw the usual "crowd." Daniel moved down the bar to stand with the one customer standing there.

"We coulda went someplace better," Cody said.

"Drink that," Clint said. "It's cold."

Cody drank some and nodded.

"Carlos wanted to buy this place," Clint said. "Did you come here with him?"

"I, uh, came with him once," Cody said.

"And then he came back with Barrett and some men," Clint said. "How many other places did he close down? Or try to close down?"

"A few," Cody said.

"Any of them owned by somebody who might have killed him?"

"Most of the men he put out of business left town," Cody said.

"What about the ones who didn't sell?" Clint asked. "How did they react to the pressure?"

"Nobody threatened him that I know of, if that's what you mean," Cody said.

Clint looked over at Daniel, wondered if the young bartender and owner of the Cactus might have reacted violently.

"Sheriff, why don't you finish your beer and wait outside?" Clint suggested.

"Again?"

"Watching my back, remember."

"Right, right." Cody drained his beer and left.

"Daniel," Clint called.

The bartender came down.

"What's your problem with Cody?"

"Is he your friend, now?" Daniel asked.

"Not at all," Clint said. "I just need him to work with me instead of trying to arrest me."

"Well, he was friends with Montalban," Daniel said. "He came here with him the first time he tried to buy me out. That lawyer had the law in his pocket."

"So you're saying Cody worked for Carlos?"

"That's the way I saw it."

"What about you, Daniel?"

"Whataya mean?"

"Well," Clint said, "somebody killed Montalban. Somebody who didn't like him."

"I didn't like 'im," Daniel said, "but I didn't kill 'im. I don't know what else to tell you."

Something occurred to Clint then, and he decided to act on it.

"Okay, Daniel. Thanks for the beer."

"Yours was on the house," Daniel said, "but you'll have to pay me for the sheriff's."

"No problem," Clint said. He put enough money on the bar for both drinks and left."

"Where to?" Cody asked.

"I want to talk to Lucinda again," Clint said. "Something just hit me."

"What?"

"I'll tell you after I check it out," Clint said. "Come on."

Chapter Thirty-Nine

When he walked into the gallery Jack asked, "Back again?"

"Is she still working?"

"She hasn't come out," the young man said.

"Okay, thanks."

Clint went to the studio again, caught Lucinda just standing in front of the easel, staring at it. It was turned so that he still hadn't seen it for himself.

"Can I come in?"

She looked at him and said, "Of course."

"Problems?" he asked.

"No," she said, "I'm just . . . thinking."

"I've been thinking, too," he said.

"About what?"

"Can I take your attention away from the painting?" he asked.

She put her brushes down, turned to face him and said, "I'm all yours."

"I reminded myself just a little while ago that when I found Carlos in here, there was no sign of a struggle of any kind," he told her. "Not here, not in the storeroom, and not in the gallery."

"Which means what?"

"That Carlos knew whoever killed him."

"They had to know him to want to kill him," she pointed out.

"Yes, but they knew him well enough for your husband to let them get close to him."

"So you're saying . . . a friend? Or me?"

"Not you," Clint said. "But did he have friends?"

"He had . . . women," Lucinda said. "One of them could have gotten near him."

"But no friends?"

She gave it some thought.

"Did he drink with anyone? Ever?"

"The mayor."

"What?"

"Before he was mayor they used to drink together," Lucinda said. "After Havestock became mayor, it changed. I believe it was because of Gertrude."

"The mayor," Clint said, giving it some thought. "He'd kill to save his mother, wouldn't he?"

"And she'd kill to save him," Lucinda said.

"Or to save his career," Clint said. "Did Carlos have an interest in being mayor?"

"Mayor," she said, "and more."

"So," Clint said, "one of them."

"How do you know which one?" Lucinda asked.

"I'll have to work it out," Clint replied.

She approached him, put her hands on his chest.

"I don't care who killed him," she said, "only that he's dead. But I want you to save yourself. Prove who did it so you can go on living without it hanging over your head."

"I will."

She stepped back.

"And then you'll leave Santa Fe?"

"Yes."

"Well," she said, "at least I'll have your portrait. I'll hold it for you until you tell me where to send it."

"Good," he said. "And when do I get to see it?"

"When it's finished." She walked back to the easel. "Now go, do what you must do."

"I'll see you after."

"And don't forget what I told you," Lucinda added. "It could have been a woman other than Gertrude Havestock."

"I'll keep that in mind."

He turned, went through the gallery and out to the street.

Chapter Forty

"This is gettin' monotonous," Cody said.

"So you want to take a more active part?" Clint asked, as they walked away from the gallery.

"Well, of course."

"Even if it means putting the mayor or his mother in a cell?"

"Are we back to that?"

"Look," Clint said, "there was no sign of a struggle. Who else would Carlos have let get that close to him?"

"How about his wife?"

"No," Clint said. "What about you?"

"Montalban and me, we weren't friends," Cody said. "He wouldn't let me walk right up and shoot him."

"How would he have stopped you?" Clint asked. "Did he carry a gun?"

"No," Cody said, "he had others do that for him."

"Like you?"

"Like Barrett."

"But you still don't think Barrett killed him?"

"No," Cody said. "And if I wanted to shift your suspicion off me, wouldn't I say yes?"

"So we're back to the mayor and his mother."

"Mrs. Havestock?" Cody said. "That's a real stretch, Adams."

They walked to the sheriff's office and went inside.

"Coffee?"

"Strong?"

"Well, it's been sittin' here since yesterday," Cody pointed out.

"Then yes."

Cody poured them each a cup, handed Clint his and took his own behind the desk with him.

"How do you intend to prove that one or the other did it?" he asked.

"Maybe," Clint said, "we can get one to prove the other did it."

"So you think whichever one is guilty, they both know?" Cody asked.

Clint sipped the coffee. It was strong enough to get the crud off of eclipse's hooves. "Maybe they don't both know. Maybe momma did it and sonny doesn't have any idea."

"Or the other way around," the sheriff said.

"Do you have the nerve to question either of them?" Clint asked. "I'm not sure the mother would even talk to me, again."

Cody took a deep breath and let it out slowly while he considered the question.

"I suppose if I stopped worryin' about my job I could question them," he said, then. "I'll tell ya, that woman scares me more than the mayor does."

"I don't blame you," Clint said. "She does seem to be the stronger of the two."

"How about if you talk to her, and I talk to the mayor?" Cody suggested.

"Like I said," Clint replied, "she might not want to talk to me again. Maybe if I force the issue, she'll reveal something. But I'd want to get her away from the office."

"And then I'll go and talk to the mayor," Cody said, "and push him a little."

Clint studied Cody's face. He still wasn't sure he could trust the lawman. After all, he had hired deputies for the specific reason of arresting him. It seemed Cody had changed sides too many times already. When would he change back, again?

"Okay," Clint said, "I guess the best way to get her away from the office is to wait until she goes home. I just need to know where she lives."

"I'll tell you how to get to their house."

"Their house?"

"Yeah," Sheriff Cody said, "the mayor lives with his mother."

***

Clint followed the directions Cody had given him to a part of town where the homes were larger and more expensive than he had seen before. Certainly much different than where Ayesha's small house was.

Once he knew where the house was, he went back to town and decided to wait until he actually saw Gertrude Havestock leave City Hall and head home. At that point, he'd follow her. When she was inside, he'd knock on the door and catch her off guard. Hopefully, she'd get mad enough to reveal something.

All he had to do was wait.

***

Sheriff Al Cody remained in his office and thought about his life. He'd been sheriff of Santa Fe for several years. Before that he'd worn a badge in other towns. What would he do if suddenly he didn't have a badge on his chest anymore?

And was that a question he really wanted to find the answer to?

Chapter Forty-One

The plan was for Clint to follow Mrs. Havestock home. The sheriff said the mayor usually stayed at the office longer than his mother. Sometimes she went home to make them supper. Other times they went out for supper. Hopefully, tonight she would go right home, and then Cody would talk to the mayor.

Cody came walking up the street as it came close to five o'clock.

"Anythin'?" he asked.

"Not yet—wait. Somebody's coming."

The front door to the City Hall building opened and Gertrude Havestock walked out.

"Okay," Clint said, "I've got her, you take him."

"Right."

Clint broke from the cover of the doorway and started following Gertrude Havestock home.

***

Sheriff Al Cody still wasn't sure he was doing the right thing, but he figured it was time for him to really start doing his job, for a change.

He entered City Hall and went up to the mayor's office. He stopped just outside and took a deep breath. One last chance to change his mind, but no, it was time to be a real lawman.

He went inside.

***

Clint watched Gertrude enter her house, gave her some time to get comfortable. Then he crossed the street, approached her front door and knocked.

When she opened the door and saw him, her face took on a hard, angry scowl that made her look even older.

"What do you want?" she demanded. "How dare you come to my house."

"That's funny. I heard it was the mayor's house, and that you lived with him."

She laughed harshly.

"It's my house, and he lives with me. What do you want, Mr. Adams?"

"To talk."

"About what?"

"The possibility that your son killed Carlos Montalban."

"Absurd!" she spat. But then she stepped back and said, "You better come in."

***

"My mother?" the mayor said, with disbelief. "You think my mother killed Carlos?"

"That's how it's starting to look."

Clint and Cody decided to employ the same tactics. Get one to defend the other.

"That's madness," Havestock said. "My mother is not a killer."

"Not even to save you?" Cody asked. "Or your career?"

"What makes you think Carlos Montalban was a threat to either of those things? Me or my career?"

"There was talk in town about him wanting to run for mayor."

"And why would I have a problem with that?" Havestock asked. "Anybody can run for mayor. It's the nature of politics." He hesitated a moment, then added, "He never would have won."

***

"What makes you say he never would've won?" Clint asked Gertrude.

"My son is the best thing that ever happened to this town," she said. "Carlos Montalban was a vile, evil, corrupt man who mistreated women. He deserved to die."

"So if your son killed him, he did this town a favor? Would that be safe to say?"

"Whoever killed him did this town a favor," she agreed, "but it wasn't my son."

***

"But you admit he mistreated women," Cody said to the mayor. "Does that include your mother?"

"He ignored my mother," Havestock said. "He didn't want to sleep with her. He only slept with lovely women, like his wife, and like . . ."

". . . his secretary?"

"Ayesha, yes," the mayor said. "She would be more likely to kill him than my mother."

Cody had to admit he was impressed with Havestock's replies to his questions. He wasn't getting angry at all at having his mother accused. He hadn't made the slightest suggestion that Cody might be risking his job with these questions.

"I'm impressed, Sheriff," Havestock said, suddenly.

"How's that?"

"You seem to be actually doing your job," the mayor answered. "That's not something I'm used to."

It took Cody a moment or two to realize he was being insulted.

"Are you working with Adams on this?" the mayor asked.

"I am," Cody said.

"And where is he while you're here?"

Cody didn't answer.

The mayor suddenly sprang up out of his chair, yelled, "Damn you!" and ran for the door.

Chapter Forty-Two

"I know what you're doing?" Gertrude Havestock said.

"Do you?"

"You're baiting me," she said. "Trying to get me angry enough to say something damning."

Clint didn't respond.

"Would you like a drink?" she asked. "I'm going to have a brandy."

"I'm not much of a brandy man."

She walked to a small, expensive looking sideboard.

"I also have whiskey."

"That I'll take."

She poured them both drinks, crossed the room and handed him his. She had changed from her work clothes into a simple dress. She had a thin, angular body, much like her face. But he thought she must have been an attractive woman twenty years ago. With her anger under control, her face had softened.

"What is it you want me to do, Mr. Adams?" she asked. "Confess that I or my son murdered Carlos Montalban? Do you think you can anger me enough to slip?"

"Let's just say I was hoping."

"I understand," she said. "You're desperate for people to stop thinking you did it, so you can leave town."

"Exactly."

"So tell me, will you accept any confession?"

He sipped his whiskey.

"No," he said, "I won't accept just anybody. I want the real killer."

"But why?" she asked. "If someone confesses, what do you care if they're telling the truth or not? You would then be able to leave Santa Fe with no shadow hanging over you."

"That's not good enough," Clint said. "I need to know the real killer will be punished."

"Is this about justice, then?"

"Yes," he said, "justice for Lucinda."

"Ah, I see," Gertrude said. "You're in love with her."

"That's not it, at all," he said. "I don't want any shadows hanging over anyone. If I leave and the killer's not found, how long do you think it'll be before people start suspecting the mayor?"

"So now you're concerned for him?" she asked. "A moment ago you were accusing him."

Clint studied her, decided to play a hunch.

"You did it."

"What?"

"Not your son," Clint said, "you."

182

She didn't respond.

"That's why you're offering me a substitute," Clint went on. "Trying to satisfy me so I'll leave and stop looking."

"You can't prove that," she said.

"No," he said, "but I don't think you pulled the trigger yourself. I think you were there, that's why there was no struggle. Carlos didn't think you were a threat. But you had somebody else there, somebody he didn't see until it was too late."

She remained silent, drank her brandy.

"All I have to do is find him," Clint said. "Maybe Barrett, or maybe somebody just like him."

"No," she said, "it was Barrett."

"So you admit it?"

"I admit I was there," she said. "I wanted Carlos to give up his idea of being mayor. I was actually going to his office to see him when he came storming out and ran to the gallery. I followed."

"With a gun?"

"No," she said, "with a man—Barrett. I decided to take him with me, just to be safe."

"But he worked for Carlos."

She smiled.

"He works for whoever pays him the most," she said. "On that day, it was me."

"So you paid him enough to kill Carlos."

"Actually, no," she said. "I didn't want him to kill him. It just . . . happened. When Carlos laughed at me and started toward me, Barrett overreacted, and shot him."

Clint studied her. There was no expression on her face, no inflection in her tone.

"You're still offering me a substitute."

"You're a very stubborn man," she said, "but I think you better leave now. I've told you all I'm going to."

"If you did take a man with you that day," Clint said, "I'll find him and get the truth."

"Good luck to you."

The front door slammed open at that point and the mayor came running in, out of breath.

"Get out!" he shouted at Clint. "Leave my mother alone. She didn't do anything."

"Take it easy, Freddie," she said. "Mr. Adams was just leaving."

That was the first time Clint had heard the mayor's first name.

"Freddie?" he said, and left.

Chapter Forty-Three

Outside Clint ran into Sheriff Cody, coming up the walk.

"I ain't never seen the mayor move so fast," he said, out of breath. "I couldn't keep up."

"You didn't miss anything," Clint said.

They continued down the walk until they were outside the gate, and stopped there so the lawman could catch his breath.

"I didn't get anything from him," he said. "He stayed real calm, until he figured out that if I was in his office, you were probably with his mother. What'd you get from her?"

"She did it."

Cody looked shocked.

"She admitted it?"

"Practically," Clint said. "She tried to tell me that Barrett was with her when she went to see Carlos in the studio. Said he overreacted and shot him."

"You believe 'er?"

"No," Clint said. "I believe she was there, and maybe she had Barrett with her, but I think she shot him, herself."

"But we can't prove it," Cody remarked.

"That's what she said."

They started walking back towards the main part of town.

"So how do we prove it?" Cody asked. "She's too smart to say anything in front of other people."

"Barrett," Clint said. "Do you know where he is?"

"I know where he might be," Cody said. "He was hidin' until I told him I didn't think he did it. Oh Jesus, she said he did it? And I put a badge on him." Cody shook his head.

"I think if we find him," Clint said, "he'll tell us she did it."

"And you'll believe 'im?"

"Sure," Clint said. "Why not? Let's give it a try and see how convincing he is."

"Okay." Cody came around from behind his desk. "There's a couple of places he might be."

***

Barrett turned the whore over onto her belly, crouched over her and brutally drove his hard cock into her. She gasped, reached up and grabbed hold of the bedpost with both hands.

"Go ahead," she said, "punish me."

She was a big girl with lots of flesh, and as he started to pound away at her, the flesh jiggled and jumped.

"Oooh, baby," she moaned, "that's it, that's it, harder . . ."

He grabbed her hips, got her up on all fours and started to give it to her harder when the door slammed open.

"What the—" he growled.

He withdrew from the girl and turned, his wet cock still pulsing and prodding at the air.

"Jesus," he said, when he saw Clint Adams.

***

As Al Cody slammed the door open, Clint looked past him, saw the huge, naked man on the bed with a meaty blonde with big, floppy breasts. The girl rolled onto her back and stared at the two men in the doorway.

"Hey, Sheriff," she said, "I'm workin'!"

"You're done, Alma," Cody said. "Did he pay you?"

"Yeah, he did."

"Then you better go downstairs," Cody said. "Me and my friend have to talk to Barrett."

She stood up, grabbed her money off the end table next to the bed, and her thin robe from the chair. But instead of putting the robe on, she just draped it over her shoulder. As she strode past them, Clint found himself unable to take his eyes off of her. She'd been at this job for a long time, was carrying a lot of extra weight, but she walked with dignity and grace.

"You can come back some other time, honey," she said to Clint, as she passed him.

Cody slammed the door shut, bringing Clint out of his trance.

"She's somethin', huh?" Barrett asked, from the bed.

"Put somethin' on, Barrett!" Cody snapped.

"Sure, Sheriff."

He got off the bed and pulled on his trousers, then sat on the edge.

"Now why'd ya come bargin' in here on my time?" he demanded.

"Mr. Adams has some questions," Cody said.

Barrett looked at Clint, who saw some trepidation in the man's eyes.

"Don't tell me," he said, "you're suspectin' me again?"

"I suspect you were there, Barrett," Clint said. "With Mrs. Havestock."

Barrett looked shocked.

"She tell ya that?"

"She did," Clint said. "And she told us that you killed Carlos."

Barrett sprang to his feet at that.

"She's a liar!"

"I believe you, Barrett," Clint said. "All you have to do is tell us the truth."

Chapter Forty-Four

"She knows where to find me when she needs me," Barrett said.

"You've worked for her before?" Clint asked.

"A lot," Barrett said. "I pretty much made my living from what she paid me, and what the lawyer paid me."

"Montalban?"

Barrett nodded.

"Did they know you were playing both ends against the middle?" Clint asked.

"I knew they didn't like each other," Barrett said, "but before that day, neither of them hired me to do anything to the other one."

"And what did she want you to do on that day?"

"Just go with 'er," Barrett said. "She said she just wanted to scare him."

"So you went to the gallery."

He nodded.

"It looked like nobody was there. I was able to force the door, and we went in the back, to the studio. It was like she knew he'd be there."

"And he was alone?" Cody asked.

"Yeah, his wife wasn't there."

"So what happened, Barrett?"

"Whataya mean what happened? She shot 'im."

"Just like that?" Clint asked. "She brought a gun."

"No, no," he said, "they argued for a while, called each other names. She told him she wasn't going to let him hurt her son's career. He laughed and called the mayor a momma's boy."

"What happened then?" Clint asked.

"She asked me to hold my gun on him."

"How did he react to that?"

"He laughed," Barrett said. "He didn't think I'd ever shoot 'im."

"And would you have?"

"Look," Barrett said, "I don't have a problem with shootin' people. But he always paid me a lot of money. I didn't wanna shoot him."

"So what happened?"

"She grabbed my gun," Barrett said. "You wouldn't think so to look at her, but she's pretty strong. She surprised me, grabbed it out of my hand, and shot him."

"Will you testify to that?"

"I don't know."

"What do you mean, you don't know?" Cody asked. "Either you will, or you won't."

"Look," Barrett said, "I've lost the money Montalban was payin' me. Now you want me to lose what Mrs. Havestock pays me."

"You could lose a lot more than that," Clint told him.

"Is that a threat?"

"It sure is."

Barrett tried to glare at Clint, but in the end, he turned his eyes away.

"Yeah, okay."

"Okay what?" Cody asked.

"I'll testify."

"And what you've told us is the truth?" Cody asked.

"Well, yeah," Barrett said. "I didn't kill 'im. She did."

Cody looked at Clint.

"Get dressed," Clint said. "We'll wait downstairs."

They went down, through the parlor full of girls waiting for customers, and outside.

"So we believe 'im," Cody said.

"Yes."

"Why?"

"I told you," Clint said. "She practically admitted it to me."

"What do we do now?"

"Toss her into a cell and contact a judge," Clint said.

"Really?" Cody asked. "You want me to put the mayor's mother in my jail?"

"I do."

"If I do that," Cody said, "it won't be my jail for much longer."

***

It was dark when they got back to the sheriff's office.

"I thought we were goin' to the mayor's house," Barrett said.

"I think we should do that in the morning," Clint said. "We'll go to City Hall and find them both there."

"Sounds like a good idea," Cody said. "And if they run tonight, that'll be even better."

"Better?" Clint asked.

"We'll know she was guilty," Cody said, "and they'll be gone."

"You think if she runs, the mayor will go with her?" Clint asked.

"He'd have to," Barrett spoke up. They looked at him. "He really is a momma's boy."

Chapter Forty-Five

They decided that Barrett would sleep in a cell, and the sheriff would sleep at his desk. Barrett didn't agree right away, so they said they wouldn't lock the door. When he was still resistant, Clint decided to sleep in the cell next to him.

In the morning they all rose, stiff and bleary-eyed.

"Let's get over to City Hall," Clint suggested.

"What about breakfast?" Barrett complained.

"After," Clint said. "Let's get this done. When Gertrude Havestock is in jail, breakfast is on me for all three of us."

"I agree," Cody said. "This might be my last day as sheriff. Might as well make it a good one."

They left the jail and headed for City Hall.

***

"Are you sure this is the way to go, Mother?" Freddie Havestock asked, from behind his desk

"There's no other way."

"What about Barrett?"

"I couldn't find him," she said, "but the others will get the job done."

"They better," the mayor said. "Are you sure they'll come?"

"I'm sure Adams will come," Gertrude said. "He'll probably bring Cody with him."

"I'll strip that badge right off his chest!" the mayor growled.

"Yes, my dear," she said, "you will, but after." She walked around behind him and placed her hands on his shoulders. "Perhaps from his dead body."

***

When Clint, Cody and Barrett entered the mayor's office, Gertrude Havestock looked up from her desk.

"Good-morning, gentlemen," she said. "We've been expecting you."

"Have you?" Clint asked.

"The mayor would like to see you," she said.

"We're not here for the mayor," Clint said. "We're here for you."

"Is that a fact?"

"Sheriff?" Clint said.

Cody swallowed, looked at Clint. For a moment, he thought the lawman would back down, but then the man straightened his shoulders.

"Mrs. Gertrude Havestock," he said, "you're under arrest for the murder of Carlos Montalban."

She stood up from her chair and extended her arms, wrists limp.

"Take me," she said. "Put on your shackles."

"That won't be necessary," Cody said. "Let's go."

"And what's he doing here?" she asked, looking at Barrett. "Is he a special deputy, again?"

"No," Clint said, "he's a witness."

"Is he?"

"According to what you said to me," Clint said, "and what he's told to the sheriff and me."

"I see," she said. "And you think a judge will believe an outlaw like him?"

"Who are you callin' an outlaw?" Barrett asked. "I ain't never stole nothin'."

"You're a killer," Gertrude said.

"That's funny, comin' from you," Barrett said. "We'll see who a judge and jury believe."

"What's going on out here?" the mayor demanded, standing in the doorway.

"Your mother is comin' with me, Mr. Mayor," Cody said. "She's under arrest."

Havestock looked at his mother, and Clint noticed as she nodded to him.

"Then take her and be done with it," the mayor said. "I've got work to do."

He turned, went into his office and closed the door.

"Well, well," Gertrude said, "I'm proud of him."

"Let's go, Mrs. Havestock," Cody said.

She marched from the room just ahead of Cody, with Barrett following. Clint didn't like how easy this had gone. Something was amiss.

He caught up to them, fell into step beside Barrett.

"What about those others?" he asked.

"What others?" Barrett asked.

"The other special deputies," Clint said. "Would they kill a lawman?"

Barrett looked at him.

"For enough money, they'd kill anybody," he said.

Clint hurried down the steps, hoping to catch Cody before he opened the front door.

"What's goin' on?" Barrett called out.

"Cody," Clint shouted, "wait!"

But it was Gertrude Havestock who didn't wait. She flung the front door wide open, and stepped aside just as the first shots rang out.

Chapter Forty-Six

The bullets struck the wall around and above the doorway. They also came through the open doorway into the interior of the hall. Clint quickly ducked for cover as the lead imbedded itself into the stairs he had been descending.

Barrett also dove for cover, but Sheriff Cody was not as lucky. Several bullets struck him in the chest, knocking him back and then down. Clint could tell he was dead, immediately.

Gertrude was crouching off to one side, watching with an excited look on her face.

"Call them off!" Clint shouted at her.

"Call who off?" she asked.

"Your men."

"What makes you think they're my men?"

He grabbed her arm.

"Don't force me to do something I don't want to do, Gertrude."

"Like what? Kill me? You wouldn't."

"No, I wouldn't," he said. "But if I walk outside with you in front of me . . ."

She suddenly looked worried.

"You wouldn't do that, either."

The shooting outside had stopped.

"I have the feeling you told them to shoot as soon as the door opened, no matter who was in the doorway. That would've taken care of the Sheriff and Barrett." He looked down. "The sheriff is dead, but not Barrett. So what will happen when you and I step out the door?"

"No, don't!" she snapped.

Clint reached down, grabbed Cody's shirt and dragged him away from the door. Then he removed his badge.

"We need a new sheriff," he said.

"You?" she demanded.

"No," he said, and tossed the badge to Barrett, who was standing on the other side of the door.

Barrett caught the badge and said, "Me?"

"You know these men," Clint said. "Call them off."

"But they're workin' for her," Barrett pointed out.

"Well," Clint said, "make them believe you are, too."

Barrett pinned the badge on.

"Okay," he said, "here goes."

He stuck one hand out the door.

"Hold your fire!" he shouted. "Ryan, is that you?"

"Barrett?" a voice called.

"That's right. I'm comin' out."

The big man took a deep breath and stepped through the door.

"See this?" he asked, pointing to the badge.

Four men stepped out into the street, their guns still drawn.

"You're the sheriff now?"

"Well, you just killed the old sheriff," Barrett said. "I'm the new one."

It occurred to Clint briefly that Barrett might turn. He also thought the four men might decide to kill the new sheriff, as well. He kept his left hand around Gertrude's thin arm, and his right hand down by his gun.

"Where's the mayor's mother?" Ryan asked.

"Inside, where it's safe."

"You workin' for her, too, Barrett?" Ryan asked.

"Why else would I be wearin' this badge?"

Suddenly, Gertrude started shouting, "Kill him! Kill him!"

Clint flung her across the room violently, hoping the move would shut her up, then stepped out to stand with Barrett as the four men began to fire, again. He pushed Barrett to one side, drew his gun and went into a crouch before firing.

The first barrage of lead went over his head, and then Barrett was up on one knee and he and Clint both returned fire. The four men in the street danced about for a few moments as hot lead hit them, and then all of them fell to the street.

Clint looked at Barrett.

"You okay?"

"Yeah," Barrett said, "thanks for comin' out when you did."

"Why don't you check and make sure the four of them are dead," Clint suggested. "I'll get Gertrude and we'll go over to the jail."

"Fine."

"Make sure you reload before you approach them," Clint added, "just in case."

He was reloading his own gun as he said it.

When he walked in, he found Gertrude Havestock crouching by her son, who was lying at the bottom of the staircase, dead.

She looked up at him, anguish on her face.

"He was coming down the stairs to see if I was all right, when the bullets came through the door."

The barrage that had gone over his head had killed the mayor.

"I guess it's all over, Gertrude."

"Yes," she said, sitting there with her son's head in her lap, "I suppose it is."

***

Once Gertrude Havestock was in jail, and the bodies had been moved to the undertaker's, Clint got Eclipse from the livery and rode over to the gallery.

As he walked into the gallery Lucinda was coming out from the back. She looked at him with relief.

"I heard the shooting," she said. "I hoped . . ."

"Sheriff Cody's dead, the mayor's dead, and the mayor's mother is in jail. She killed Carlos."

Lucinda nodded.

"So it's all over?" she asked.

"The town might need to elect a new sheriff, but yeah, it's over."

"And you're leaving?"

"Right now," he said.

"Wait," she said, "before you go, come in the back."

"Lucinda—"

"Your portrait is finished."

"Oh."

He followed her into the studio, where she turned the easel around. He was amazed at how lifelike his portrait looked, and yet it didn't.

"What do you think?"

"It's beautiful," he said.

"I'll keep it here," she said. "You can contact me if and when you decide you want it."

"We agreed on a price," he said, digging into his pocket.

"Never mind," she said. "You've done enough for this town." She approached him, kissed his cheek and said, "Good-bye, Clint."

"'bye."

He went outside and mounted up. It wasn't exactly true that he was leaving right "now." First, he rode over to Ayesha's house to let her know she could come outside, and that turned into a long goodbye.

Coming November 27, 2019

THE GUNSMITH
453
Deadly Heirloom

For more information
click here: www.SpeakingVolumes.us

On Sale Now!
THE GUNSMITH
450

For more information
visit: www.SpeakingVolumes.us

Coming December 15, 2019

Lady Gunsmith
8
Roxy Doyle and the Silver Queen

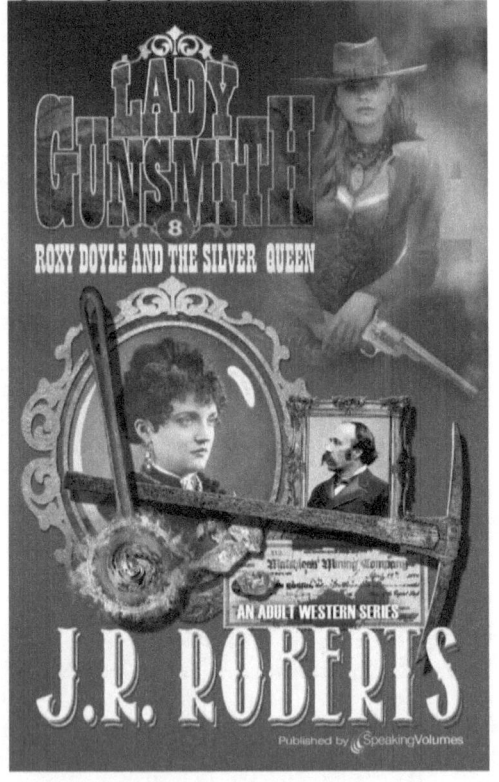

**For more information
click here:** www.SpeakingVolumes.us

On Sale Now!

Lady Gunsmith *series*
Books 1-6

**For more information
visit:** www.SpeakingVolumes.us

On Sale Now!

ANGEL EYES *series*
by Award-Winning Author
Robert J. Randisi (J.R. Roberts)

For more information
visit: www.SpeakingVolumes.us

On Sale Now!

TRACKER *series*
by Award-Winning Author
Robert J. Randisi (J.R. Roberts)

On Sale Now!

MOUNTAIN JACK PIKE *series*
by Award-Winning Author
Robert J. Randisi (J.R. Roberts)

For more information
visit: www.SpeakingVolumes.us

50% Off
Audiobooks